THE BURDEN OF LOVING A BROKEN MIND

MICHELLE BRUNETTE

FriesenPress
One Printers Way
Altona, MB R0G 0B0
Canada

www.friesenpress.com

First Edition — 2025

Disclaimer: This novel contains sensitive content that may be triggering to some readers. Topics include: *Suicide ideation and attempts, depression and mental illness, acts of violence, domestic and sexual abuse, grief/loss.* **Reader discretion is advised**. If you or someone you know is struggling with mental health or are a victim of abuse, please consider the following resources:
International Mental Health Helpline: HelpGuide.org/find-help
Domestic and Sexual Violence Support: NoMoreDirectory.org

ISBN
978-1-03-833116-8 (Hardcover)
978-1-03-833115-1 (Paperback)
978-1-03-833117-5 (eBook)

1. *FICTION, THRILLERS, DOMESTIC*

Distributed to the trade by The Ingram Book Company

To the strongest and most admirable person I know:

Thank you for brightening our path
through the darkness with your light.

Je t'aime, Mom.

PART ONE

Chapter 1

1985

"Do you know that guy?"

I break eye contact with the man across the room, and turn to my sister. "No. I mean, not really. I know *of* him. I think he went to our high school for a year. One grade below yours, I believe."

Robin shrugs. "I'm certain I would've noticed someone as good looking as him at our school."

"Probably not," I reply, laughing. "You were always so distracted in high school that you couldn't even keep up with a conversation. You were so in love with Rodney that he consumed your every thought."

She nods in agreement and smirks. "You're right." Robin is three years older than me, but sometimes I feel like I'm the one to offer her sisterly advice.

She had her first boyfriend, Rodney, when she was only fifteen years old. He was significantly older than her, and he treated her terribly when they were alone, but he masked it with charm whenever he was around us. He destroyed her self-esteem.

Robin is beautiful. She has long, thick chestnut hair and a perfect smile. She wasn't popular in high school, but that wasn't due to lack of good looks. She was shy around guys, and she never put herself out there. She wouldn't go to parties or join any clubs. She had several close girl friends, but she didn't expand her social circle beyond that. When she started dating Rodney, we were so happy she had found someone. But that was before I learned the details of their disturbing relationship.

Robin met Rodney where she worked at the local supermarket. He was her manager, which already created a weird power dynamic between them. He was also twenty-five years old, and she was barely past the age of consent. Due to his position over her at work and the ten-year age gap, I couldn't help but feel like he took advantage of her innocence. But when I would tell my parents about how wrong it felt, my mom would always say the same thing.

"I know, honey. But it's legal. Your father and I got married when I was only sixteen, and he was twenty. At least she's finally showing interest in boys."

"Boys?" I replied. "Mom, that's not a boy. That's a man! This is wrong!"

It was especially hard for my parents to understand. They were born in the early 1920s, and they grew up in a generation where child brides weren't uncommon. As long as it was legal, it was fine, according to my parents and the rest of society. Even at twelve years old, I felt that it wasn't right. Now that I'm nineteen, it feels even more disgusting.

It took a long time for Robin to realize she needed to leave him. He cheated throughout their relationship with different young girls. He always made her feel like she wasn't good enough, like he had some kind of power over her due to his "maturity and wisdom," as he would put it. In reality, he was just a huge asshole. He preyed on innocent young girls because no woman his age wanted to deal with his trashy personality.

I overheard one of their conversations once. Rodney didn't know I was home from babysitting, and I caught him yelling horrendous things to her.

"I'm the one who gets to decide what we do. Not you! I'm the adult here! You think you can have your own opinions? I own you. The only reason you have any kind of value is because of me."

Of course, me being me, I leaped to her defence and attempted to expose him.

"How dare you speak to Robin that way? You might be older, but you're a piece of shit. Why don't you go find a woman your own age? Oh, that's right. You can't. Because no grown woman on this earth would ever take this bullshit, so you take advantage of young girls instead. That's the only way you're ever going to feel like you have any kind of worth."

I couldn't tell if my words even affected him. If they did bother him, he did an amazing job at hiding it because he just laughed. "You're so cute, Gen. Trying to defend your big sister. There's no need. She can take care of herself." He tapped the top of Robin's head, degrading her further.

"You're too young to understand, Gen," Robin said. Her eyes were red and puffy, like she'd been crying for hours. "Let me handle this." She dragged him into her bedroom and shut the door in my face.

The truth was that she was the one who didn't understand. Robin had no idea that she could do so much better than him. It broke my heart.

I never gave up on trying to free her from that terrible man. Finally, a year after I witnessed that argument, I was able to gather proof that he was cheating on her with this other girl who was a year younger than Robin. When I think of it, it still leaves a bad taste in my mouth. I hope he's in prison or something now and is finally getting what he deserves.

"He keeps looking over here," Robin says, interrupting my thoughts. "Is he looking at me or you? Maybe he recognizes me from high school."

Ever since Rodney, Robin has a newfound sense of confidence. I'm so proud of her. Just one of those "little sister acting as big sister" things, I guess. There's a chance he's looking at her, except it's painfully obvious that he's been making eye contact with me since I entered the pub. His gaze had been practically burning into my skin, his eyes scanning up and down my body from the moment we sat down at the opposite end of the room. Regardless, I entertain her comment.

"Maybe. You should go find out," I say.

She laughs. "There's no way I have the guts to do that. If he wants to talk to me, he'll have to approach me. I don't chase."

I love seeing this side of Robin. It comes out more when she's had a few whisky sours. After seeing how badly Rodney crushed her spirit, it's good to see she knows her worth.

Robin and I are opposites in many ways. She's a lot more reserved than I am. She's the kind of girl who would rather stay in and read a book while I'm always looking for a good time. I've had to drag her out almost every weekend since I reached legal drinking age.

Even though I'm more outgoing than Robin, I've never had a boyfriend. I like to think it's by choice. After seeing how miserable she was throughout the majority of her high school years, I pledged not to date in high school. I didn't want the memories of my youth to be tainted by a meaningless relationship that probably wouldn't last. I still stand by my decision. While my friends were getting their hearts broken, I was having the best time ever. There's no better feeling than having the freedom of doing whatever you want. Of course, it got lonely at times, but that was a small price to pay for having peace.

Now, after all these years of being single, I'm finally ready to put myself out there. I want to find love. I've got so much of it to give, and I feel like I'm finally mature enough to handle the weight of a real relationship.

"Oh my God, he's coming over here."

I turn toward where Robin is looking. The tall, dark-haired man who has been looking in our direction all night is walking through the crowd of people on the dance floor toward our table. As he approaches, I notice a smirk on his face. He looks confident, as he should. He's so gorgeous, it's almost surreal.

"Hello, Genevieve Daley." He holds his hand out. I stare at him, surprised he knows my name, then reach my hand toward his.

"Hello. It's nice to meet you." I wait for him to tell me his name, my face growing hot from feeling his eyes on me.

"Wallace Browne," he says with a kind smile.

There's no denying that he's handsome. I try not to look nervous. I can tell that Robin is trying too, but she's not doing a good job. I hope I'm being less obvious than her.

"I couldn't help but notice that you haven't had a drink in your hand all night," he says. "Would you allow me to buy you one?"

"Oh, I'm actually not drinking tonight. Robin and I take turns being the designated driver." I chuckle, looking toward Robin so that he acknowledges her.

"Oh, what a great system you two have. It's nice to meet you as well, Robin. I'm sorry; I was so distracted by your friend that I didn't have the decency to introduce myself to you."

Robin's face turns red. I can't tell if it's from embarrassment or irritation.

"She's my sister. And it's fine," she says with an annoyed tone. He doesn't seem bothered by the fact that he may have offended her.

"You've both been blessed with great genes." He grins, then looks back at me. Robin's expression softens from the compliment. "So, how about that drink?" he asks. "I can buy you a soda or something."

He takes my hand and pulls me toward the bar. Even though I'm hesitant to leave Robin, I'm compelled to follow him. "I'll be right back," I mouth to her. She nods, her arms crossed, an eyebrow raised, and a suggestive look on her face. I feel bad for leaving her alone, but she doesn't seem upset. She's probably happy that I'm finally getting some action.

Seconds later, I see a man approach her, and she smiles. She must think he's attractive because she twirls her hair and giggles while speaking with him. I'm relieved because now I can focus on the sexy man who is pulling me across the room. This is so exciting!

Chapter 2

"So, how do you know my name?" I ask Wallace as he pays for our drinks. The bartender has a weird look on his face as he gives Wallace his change. I assume he's probably just tired of working around drunk people all of the time.

"It turns out, we have something in common," Wallace says. "My older brother is friends with yours." He smiles and wraps his arm around my shoulders. I'm surprised I've never heard of him before. "You came up in a conversation a few months ago. Greg, my older brother, told me about how Dan's sister is the first person in his family to go to university. He and my mother were talking about how they didn't understand why you would choose a career over finding a man to support you and allow you to stay at home right after high school. I, however, think it's admirable for you to prioritize your independence. After I asked for your name, I looked you up in the yearbook, since I knew some people with the last name Daley who went to Dame Hart College the same year I was there. It turns out you were in grade nine when I was in grade twelve. You look so young in that picture, but I still recognized you as soon as you walked through the door tonight."

He leans closer to me, and whispers in my ear. "And you've grown up into the most breathtaking woman I've ever seen."

Shivers go up my spine. No man has ever complimented me like that before. At least not a man *this* attractive. It's nice that he's not threatened by my ambitions, although it sounds like his family has the same old-school opinions as mine.

"Thank you," I reply, trying to control the tremble in my voice. Those are the only words I can get out before he grabs my waist and pulls me against him. Our faces are inches apart. I notice that he's staring at my lips. My heart feels like it's beating out of my chest. As our lips are about to connect, the bartender interrupts the moment.

"Two gin and tonics," he says in a cold tone while passing the drinks to Wallace.

"Why does he sound so mad?" I whisper.

Wallace shrugs. "I don't know. Probably because I never tip him." He laughs as he pulls me away from the bar.

Before I can respond to what he said, he walks me to the dance floor and passes me my drink. I take a sip and try not to make a weird face. Gin and tonic is disgusting. "I told you that I'm not supposed to drink tonight!" I shout above the music.

"One drink should be fine," he says. "If not, I'll pay for a cab for you and your sister."

I smile when he says that. *How considerate,* I think. I take another sip of my drink, then I reach up and wrap my arms around his neck. *God, he's so tall.*

His dark brown eyes meet mine. "Now, can we go back to the moment before that bartender rudely interrupted us?" he asks, his lips brushing my ear.

"Maybe he wouldn't have interrupted the moment if you had the decency to tip the man," I say with a teasing smirk. He laughs, then looks down at my lips.

"I promise I'm a good tipper. Except when it comes to that guy. He's always trying to ruin my fun." He places one hand on the small of my back and cups my cheek with the other. "But I'm not going to let him ruin it this time." His lips press into mine.

At the end of the night, he calls us a cab.

Chapter 3

It's been a week since that night, and Wallace still hasn't called. I didn't go home with him, which might be why he decided he doesn't want to see me again. I really wanted to, but I couldn't leave Robin behind.

After that electrifying kiss, we spent the rest of the evening all over each other. Robin spent her time with one of his friends, Justin, but it didn't seem like they hit it off. They didn't even exchange numbers. Wallace and I, on the other hand, were enthralled with each other's company. He ended up buying me five drinks in total, and at the end of the night, he bought pizza for all of us. He also had the cab driver drop off Robin and me first to ensure we made it home safe, even though his house was a lot closer to the pub. He was the perfect gentleman. However, I'm wondering how he has all this money to spend, seeing as he's a student, just like me. I know he's living at home, and

I'm renting, but he seems totally unbothered with how much he spends. He must have rich parents or something.

After how much attention he gave me that night, I thought for sure he would call right away to make plans with me. I suppose I have to accept that it was just a one-time thing.

"I can't believe we have three classes together this semester!" Ramon says to me as we walk across campus. Ramon is my best friend from high school. He's also the sweetest kid you'll ever meet. We met in grade nine in photography class. When our teacher told everyone to team up and take portraits of one another, he asked if we could team up. "I'll make those green eyes pop!" he said with such confidence as he took my picture.

Back then, he was a short, cute kid with chubby cheeks. He's definitely grown into a man since then. He towers me, and his baby face is long gone. He's quite handsome, but I've always seen him as just a friend.

"I know!" I reply. "I'm so happy. I'm also glad I won't be alone during my first week here. I'm so nervous. I can't believe we're here."

It's our first year of university. After graduating from Dame Hart, Ramon and I are practically the only two students in our grade who didn't go to a college or university out of town. I guess we're the only ones who appreciate the charm of our small town.

"Think about it," Ramon says. "In just four years, you're going to be a teacher, and I'm going to be a software engineer. We're going to be such successful adults." His dark blue eyes are filled with hope.

"I can't wait," I reply. I've wanted to be a teacher for as long as I can remember. There's something endearing about the way teachers dedicate their time to their students. I always admired the strength and patience of my teachers growing up. I hope I'll be able to inspire children as much as my teachers have inspired me.

"So, Wallace still hasn't called you?" Ramon asks, interrupting my thoughts.

I shake my head. "No. I guess we didn't connect as well as I thought we did."

"Well, maybe he was so taken by your beauty and charm, he's afraid he isn't good enough to be in your presence again." Ramon laughs as he runs his hand through his light brown hair.

I give him a playful shove. "Yes, I'm sure that's what it is."

Chapter 4

"Someone is knocking at the door!" Robin yells from across the apartment. I groan as I get off the couch. She's always too afraid to answer the door. She says it gives her anxiety. I think it's just an excuse, so she doesn't have to get up.

"I got it!" I yell back. I fix my hair in the bathroom mirror before heading to the front door. I open it and see Wallace with a bouquet of flowers and an apologetic look on his face.

"Wallace, these are beautiful!" I smile at him as he hands them to me. "Thank you. Do you want to come in?" I ask.

He shakes his head. "No, thank you. I have somewhere to be in about ten minutes. I just wanted to stop by and let you know I lost the paper you wrote your phone number on the night we met. I contemplated all week stopping by your apartment, but I figured I might run into you on campus. I realized after the first day back that our classes are in two different buildings, so those chances were slim. I couldn't stop thinking about the evening we spent together, and regardless of how creepy it seemed, I decided to knock on your door, so I could ask you out on an official date." He smiles confidently. He's so charming, he could have said anything and I probably would have agreed to go on a date with him.

"Yes. I'd love to go on a date with you," I say with a bit too much enthusiasm.

He seems pleased by my answer. "Great. How about tomorrow? I can pick you up at seven."

"Perfect. See you then."

He takes my hand and kisses it. I feel like I'm going to melt away from his touch.

"I can't wait," I say as I close the door, my heart racing.

...

"I don't know how I feel about him." Robin says to me as I prepare for my date with Wallace.

"Why do you say that?" I ask while applying shiny rose-coloured lip gloss that matches my dress. "I'm not sure. He just seems a little too perfect. He has endless charm, endless compliments, and endless money. It's all kind of odd. No man in this town is that kind. There's no way."

Since her breakup with Rodney, she's convinced every man is a cheating asshole. I, on the other hand, want to try and have faith in men at least once before I give up on them forever. I mean, I definitely need to lose my virginity first.

"Robin, I'm sure good men exist. How are we ever gonna know if we don't try?"

She shrugs. "I guess you're right. I should give him a chance. He did redeem himself quite well after he basically ignored my existence when he first introduced himself to you."

I recall the moment when he offered a drunken apology to Robin later on in the night and offered to buy her a drink to make up for it. His charms still work while he's intoxicated, it seems.

"Anyways, just be careful Gen. He seems like a great guy, but you don't really know him. This is your first real connection with someone, so I don't want you to go into it blindly. Don't move too quickly. If he's worth it, he'll have patience."

It's nice to hear how much my sister cares for me. It feels different being on the receiving end of advice and concern. I will be careful going forward. I saw how Robin's breakup affected her. I wouldn't want to go through the same thing. I'm certain, however, that Wallace is different from Rodney.

Chapter 5

Since our first date, Wallace and I have spent almost every single day together. I've done more things in the last three weeks than I've done in my entire life. We've gone on road trips, we've been to parties, we've gone to fancy restaurants, and so much more. I didn't think it was possible for someone to have this much energy to do so many activities in so little time. It's thrilling. The more time I spend with Wallace, the more exciting life gets.

"Wow, you finally show up," Ramon says as I sit down next to him in the auditorium.

"I'm sorry! I've been... busy," I reply. I can't help but smirk.

"Too busy to show up for class? Gen, this is your future! You can't throw it away for your new boyfriend." He's clearly annoyed with my poor choices recently. I've never seen him so concerned before.

"I've only missed a few classes, Ramon. It's not a *crime*." My comment is on brand, considering we're currently on the subject of criminal acts and defiance in the sociology class we're attending. He just looks at me, not biting on my attempt at being funny. "Okay, okay. I'm sorry," I say. "I'll stop missing class. It's just that I haven't been sleeping much. Wallace and I stay up almost all night when we're together, so I often sleep through my alarm."

He raises an eyebrow, looking concerned. "Is that normal?"

"Is what normal?"

"That Wallace keeps you up all night when you're together. Isn't he a third-year student? Doesn't he have classes too?"

"Yes, he's in ConEd like me. I don't know; I swear this guy never seems to need any sleep."

Ramon frowns. "That's odd," he says, a suspicious tone in his voice. "Regardless, he's a bad influence if he keeps you up all night. You're in first year. You don't want to fail simply for being careless. No man is worth that, Gen. Believe me." He sounds serious. Ramon has always been protective of me. When he gives me advice, I take it. His dark blue eyes have a hint of worry in them.

"Don't worry Ramon. I won't let Wallace get in the way of my future career. I couldn't handle you having that kind of accomplishment without me by your side."

Ramon smiles and shakes his head. "You better not," he says.

Chapter 6

After class, I decide to visit my mom and dad. Daniel, our older brother, said he was going to be there, and I want to talk to him about Wallace.

I open the front door and enter the hallway. "Hi, Mom! Hi, Dad!" I say as I walk in, making my presence known. They get up from their chairs in the living room to greet me.

"Hi honey, it's so nice to see you!" My mom's eyes light up as she gives me a tight hug. She's such a small woman, but she gives the strongest, most comforting hugs. It's one of the things I love most when I come home to visit.

My dad gives me a kiss on the cheek. "Hi baby, we've missed you," he says.

"I've missed you both so much!" I reply. "I know it's only been a few months since I moved out, but I miss Mom's home-cooked meals so much. Mine and Robin's cooking doesn't even compare." They both laugh.

"Come, take a seat." My dad motions toward the living room. I follow him and Mom, then take a seat on the large sofa.

Soon after, Daniel comes out of the bathroom. He greets me and then takes a seat next to me. "How are Linda and the kids?" I ask him. Daniel has been married to Linda for three years. They have one three-year-old daughter, Leona, named after our mother, and one eight-month-old son, Ruben.

"They're great," he says. "They keep me busy, but they make me so happy." As he continues talking about them, smiling the entire time, I think about how excited I am to start a family one day.

"So, honey, how's your first year of university going so far?" my mother asks. She was one of the many members of my family who tried to discourage me from going to uni. She told me that spending that kind of money on school was ridiculous, and that I should get a job straight out of high school like Robin did. My mother means well, but she always manages to subconsciously compare my siblings and me. It often started fights between us when we were younger or created jealousy.

"It's going really well!" I lie. I'm not going to admit to my parents that I've missed quite a few classes already, which resulted in two failed grades so far. "By the way, I wanted to let you all know I'm seeing someone." It's a way to change the subject from my academic pursuits.

"That's wonderful! Who's the lucky man?" my mom asks, excited. My dad stays silent with an unreadable expression on his face. He must not be pleased to hear that his youngest daughter has started dating, even though I'm nineteen years old.

"His name is Wallace. Wallace Browne. Dan, he mentioned that you're friends with his brother Greg?"

"Yes... I am," Daniel replies, giving me a concerned look. "How serious is your relationship with him?"

His question catches me off guard. I haven't really thought of that. We haven't officially told each other that we're exclusive, I just thought Wallace and I were both on the same page with our intentions. I mean, we've been spending almost every day together. That must mean something special to him.

"I'm not sure, I don't believe we've talked about it. It's still fairly new," I say.

"I see," he replies. Daniel's expression changes, and he becomes quiet after that. I assume he has something he wants to tell me, but he doesn't want to say it in front of my parents. I can't wait for the visit to end, so I can speak to him alone.

...

After a few hours, we say goodbye to our parents and we make our way to the driveway, standing in front of our vehicles. "Okay. Tell me what's going on. What do you know about Wallace?" I ask.

He looks down at me while rubbing his thumb across his lips. It looks like he's contemplating whether or not he should tell me the truth. "I don't know anything for certain. I haven't spoken to Greg in a long time."

I'm shocked by this revelation. "What? Why? I thought you were friends!"

"We were still friends up until three years ago," he says. "The truth is, over the last few years, he changed. When we were younger, we had so much fun. He was the kind of person who would never stop. He was constantly on the go. Whether it was with sports, extracurriculars, or girls, he was always doing something productive and exciting. Not only that, he was the best at everything he did.

"However, after we graduated from high school, something strange happened to him. It was like something inside of him switched off. He disappeared for months, and I had no way of reaching him." He shakes his head, as if he's still stunned from the experience all these years later. "I tried going over to his house, but his mother, Rhea, refused to let me in. She would always tell me that he wasn't feeling well and that he would call when he felt better. Except it took *months* for him to feel better.

"When the time finally came, he reached out to me, and we went out for drinks. The first time I saw him again, he was unrecognizable. He had lost so much weight, his face looked sunken. When I asked about what happened, he refused to explain."

I have a hard time believing what Dan is telling me. How can someone go months without leaving their house?

"Once we started hanging out again, it was as if he was back to his old self, but his personality appeared to be heightened. He went right back to being the busybody he'd always been, but it was as if his mind couldn't shut off. He would barely sleep. And eventually, he became reckless. Dangerous, even. He started drinking way too much and got into heavy drugs. One time he got into a car accident in Orillia and almost killed a woman and her children. When they found him, he was passed out, completely wasted, in the driver's seat. It was only eight in the evening.

"It was after that incident that I decided to cut all ties with him. Linda had just given birth to Leona, and I didn't want that kind of influence anywhere near my wife or child. The craziest part is, it's as if he never even noticed that I was suddenly missing from his life. No calls, no nothing. It was as if our friendship had never even existed."

I had no idea that Dan had been through that. Him and I hadn't been close growing up, but I feel like that's something either he or my parents would have talked about when it happened.

"I'm sorry you went through that, Dan. It must've been hard to lose such a close friend." I give him a hug. He remains stiff, but he hugs me back. He's never been the kind of sibling to show much affection.

"Thanks, Gen. Anyways, the reason I'm telling you this is to warn you about what you might be getting yourself into. Obviously, Wallace isn't the same person as Greg. He doesn't necessarily share the same... *peculiarities.*" He scratches the back of his head. "Just be careful going forward. What happened with his brother shouldn't stop you from finding happiness with Wallace. If he's a good man, he deserves a fair chance."

He smiles. I nod in agreement, but my head is spinning. I've been dating Wallace for three weeks, and he hasn't mentioned his family at all. I understand if he would be hesitant to share something so heavy with me. Besides, his brother's life isn't any of my business. I just hope he isn't hiding anything from me.

I say goodbye to Dan and then get into my car. As I drive back to my apartment, a disturbing thought crosses my mind, making my heart sink. If Dan hasn't spoken to Greg in three years, how the hell did Wallace know I was the first person in my family to go to university?

Chapter 7

"Why did you lie to me?" I ask Wallace, trying to mask the fear in my voice. It's been a week since my conversation with Dan. I haven't had a chance to see Wallace because of midterms coming up. I have started taking school seriously, especially after the promise I made to Ramon.

"What are you talking about?" Wallace asks, his dark eyes piercing mine.

"You said that you heard about me because your brother is friends with mine. It turns out, Dan hasn't spoken to Greg in three years." I cross my arms and shift farther back into my seat. I didn't want to have this conversation in a restaurant, but I also didn't want to have it back at my apartment, where Robin would definitely be listening in.

Wallace looks at me with a confused expression. "I didn't lie to you, Genevieve, I swear. That's what Greg told me! I just assumed he got that information from your brother. I had no idea they were no longer friends."

He leans across the table, and grabs my hand, rubbing his thumb back and forth near my wrist. "I'm sure there's a reasonable explanation. It's a relatively small town, and I'm sure there are mutual friends somewhere who may have shared that information with Greg. Regardless, I promise I didn't lie to you. I certainly didn't lie about the part where I said how much I admire you."

He gives me a flirty smile and kisses the top of my hand, then places my palm on his cheek. There's sincerity in his voice. I can tell that he's telling the truth. I set aside the uneasy feeling. Wallace is right. That information could have been shared with anyone. Robin has many friends around the same age as Wallace and his brother. Maybe she's the reason Greg found that out about me. I still wonder why my name would come up in a conversation in the Browne household, especially since Greg and Daniel's friendship ended in such a weird way.

I push those thoughts out of my mind and return my attention to Wallace. He looks good tonight. He's wearing a black button-down shirt with the sleeves rolled up. His dark hair is styled perfectly, and he's clean shaven. I can smell his aftershave from across the table.

"I want you to know you're really special to me," Wallace says. After hearing Robin calling me Gen last week, he thought she said *Gem*, and he's been calling me that ever since. "You are a gem, Genevieve. It's why it's so perfect. My little Gem," he said.

"You're special to me too, Wallace. These last few weeks have been amazing."

He smiles at my response. "I just want to make it clear that my intention is to marry you one day," he says. My mouth falls open. Did he actually just say that? I cover my mouth with my hand. "I'm serious, Gem," he continues. "There's something about you. I think we're meant to be together."

I can't prevent a huge smile from forming on my face. Despite the warnings from Robin and Dan, Wallace has proven to be nothing but a gentleman with the right intentions. I think he's good for me.

"I guess we'll just have to see," I say with a playful grin. He pushes himself out of his side of the booth and slides in beside me.

"Oh yes, we'll see indeed," he replies. Then he grabs me by the waist and leans in to kiss me.

Chapter 8

1986

Wallace and I have been in a relationship for four months now. In that time, I have fallen hard for him. We spend all of our free time together, and we've had so many amazing moments.

A few months back, he surprised me with a weekend getaway in Montreal for my birthday, where he officially asked me to be his. He set up a romantic date with flowers, champagne, and chocolates. He brought me to one of the fanciest rooftop restaurants in the area that had a view of the entire city. The five-star hotel where we stayed had rooms that were bigger than my entire apartment. It felt like I was living a dream.

We spent Christmas together. He met my family, and I met his. My parents love him, as I predicted. He's such a charmer.

I met his mother and his older sister. His father passed away when he was young, and Greg lives out of town for work and couldn't make it home for the holidays this year. His mother is kind but reserved. She isn't the talkative type. His sister, Candace, is nice, but she seems like the kind of person to talk badly behind a person's back. I act carefully around her. It's not the kind of family I picture myself being incredibly close to. But that doesn't matter. Wallace treats me like royalty. He's worth it even if it means I won't have the greatest in-laws.

We also spent New Year's Eve together. Robin and I threw a small gathering at our apartment with a few of our close friends. At midnight, while everyone cheered for the new year ahead, Wallace and I were only paying attention to each other. Completely unaware of the chaos surrounding us. It was as if we were the only two people in the room. He kissed me so passionately. It was the best kiss we had ever shared.

As his lips parted from mine, he gazed at me. "I'm in love with you, my Gem. I'm in love with every part of you. I can't wait for what this new year will bring for us. I love you so much."

When he leaned in for another kiss, my heart was beating so fast, butterflies filled my stomach as I took in the most beautiful words a man had ever said to me.

"I love you too Wallace. So much," I replied. I was overwhelmed with joy and excitement. He was such a perfect boyfriend that I never would've expected what came just a few weeks later.

...

The signs were subtle at first, but I would have recognized them if it hadn't been on cloud nine for months on end. He tried so hard to hide the surprisingly dark part of himself. He did such a good job that it wasn't until I was madly in love with him that the darkness had finally overcame him.

The depression.

I had noticed he had become less energetic over the last few months, but I thought he was finally coming down from the high of our new relationship. He was still the same caring, loving Wallace; he was just slightly calmer than when I first met him. He no longer kept me up all night with him to party or took me on spontaneous road trips in the middle of the week. That was a good thing, actually, because it allowed me to focus on my studies. Only when he stopped calling me altogether did I realize something was seriously wrong.

"What's happening to him?" I ask Candace, while taking a seat on their living room couch. I'm at Wallace's house to find out why he hasn't called me in over a week. His mother is out with her friends, so it's just Candace and me in the room. Wallace is in his bedroom downstairs.

"He dropped out of university," she says.

My eyes widen. "What? He only has a few months left before he can get into teacher's college! Why would he do that?" I shake my head in disbelief.

"He couldn't do it anymore. Every day, it was harder and harder for him to get out of bed. He became incredibly anxious, had panic attacks, and would barely leave the house unless it was to spend time with you. He dropped out about two weeks ago. He failed his latest exam, and he was no longer able to keep up with the rest of his class."

I can't tell how she's feeling at this moment, but she doesn't seem shocked that this has happened to her brother.

"He was also drowning in credit card debt." She gives me a critical look, as if she's insinuating that I have something to do with it. "He was unable to make his payments after he lost his part-time job at the school."

I can't believe all of this was happening without me knowing.

"Our mother had to pay off all of his debt, so he wouldn't have to declare bankruptcy."

I'm speechless. I can't even process what she's telling me. When I'm finally able to speak, I try my best not to sound like I'm panicking. "How can something like this happen? He would never allow me to pay for anything whenever we would go out. He told me he received an inheritance from his father from when he passed away and that he had more than enough money to cover such lavish expenses. I never would have allowed him to spoil me like that if I knew he was struggling!"

Candace appears unfazed.

"If he was having a hard time with school, why didn't he tell me? I would've helped him!" I'm sobbing now. I can't believe the man I love was going through so much, and I didn't even notice.

"He was ashamed, Genevieve. He did everything he could to hide that part of himself from you." She puts a hand on my shoulder in an attempt to comfort me. "He wasn't able to ask for help because he had no idea how to navigate what he was going through. He also has a hard time accepting that he has the same illness as Greg."

I had forgotten what Dan told me about Greg. It all makes so much sense now. I would be terrified to experience the same symptoms after seeing my own brother go through his own horrible experience. I understand how he would feel ashamed. Depression and mental illness are rarely talked about, always kept hidden behind closed doors. It's especially uncommon to hear about men struggling with such issues.

"Can I see him?" I ask, wiping the tears off of my face.

"You can try. He hasn't come out of his room in two days."

Candace gets up and goes to the kitchen. She fills a glass with water, then brings it back into the living room and hands it to me. "Try to get him to drink some water. I'm afraid he's just letting himself die in there."

I take the glass and make my way down to the basement where his bedroom is, unsure what I'll find.

Chapter 9

I knock on his door. "Hey, it's Gem. Can I come in?" No answer. I knock again, slightly louder. "Babe, please let me come in. I need to make sure you're okay." Still nothing. I try the doorknob, but it's locked. Remembering the bobby pin I have in my hair, I take it out and let my bangs fall to the sides of my face. I push it into the lock, and it pops open almost immediately. I open the door and step inside his bedroom, only to stop short.

The place is a mess. Clothes and trash are everywhere. I've never seen such a cluttered room. It takes a moment before I spot Wallace underneath all the trash that's piled on top of his bed.

"Oh, Wallace," I mutter in disbelief, trying to hide the disgust in my voice. "Babe, please drink this water for me." I approach his bed, trying not to gag as the smell of rotting food and dirty laundry enter my nose. I don't understand how someone can stay in such conditions for hours on end.

He finally pulls the covers off, exposing his bare chest. How did I not notice how slim he's gotten? I only saw him a week ago. He looks sickly. I try to hide the stunned expression that I know is all over my face.

"I didn't want you to see me like this," he says. He sits up and takes the glass of water from my hand. He takes a sip, then his eyes fill with tears. "I've been trying to tell you for weeks, but you're always so full of life that I didn't have the heart to risk stripping that away from you."

I take his hand in mine. "Wallace. I love you. You don't have to keep this sort of thing from me. I can help you. We can find you resources. Anything to help you get out of this state. Please, you have to let me help you." Tears roll down my face again.

"You don't understand, Genevieve. I can barely get out of bed. I can hardly move. Everything is so dark." He starts crying and throws himself in my arms. "There's no way for me to escape the darkness. It's as if it has become a part of me," he manages to say between sobs.

My heart breaks, seeing him in this state. I can't even imagine what he's feeling at this moment. To have your own mind turn against you must be the most painful thing of all.

"I'm here for you, Wallace. I'll always be here for you. I won't give up on you." I rub his back, trying to soothe him. "We'll find a way to get you better." I have no idea how, but I'm determined to help him, no matter what it takes.

...

After about an hour, I manage to get him to go take a shower and brush his teeth. I offer to help him if he needs to, but he says he'll be fine. While he's in the bathroom, I pick up the trash, change his sheets, vacuum the room, and put his dirty clothes in the hamper with the rest of the laundry.

While cleaning, I find a photo under his bed. It's a picture of him and his dad. Wallace appears to be about five years old. They're both smiling. Did his father suffer from depression too? Is that how he died?

As I place the photo on the desk next to Wallace's bed, my mind returns to how Wallace told me his dad left him a large inheritance, which is a lie. Why would he lie to me about having so much money? He knows I don't care about that kind of thing. I can't mention it to him in his current state, though. I have to leave it be. I can't start questioning everything he does or says. So what if he lied about having lots of money? All I care about is that he gets better, so we can continue our wonderful life together. I must be patient. I must love him through this.

Chapter 10

It's been three days since I discovered that Wallace is struggling with depression. After leaving his house that day, I went straight to the campus library to find some information on depression.

I spent hours that night looking through different books about psychiatric disorders. None of them described the symptoms that Wallace was experiencing until I found a book published in the 1970s titled *The Stages of Manic Depression*. I decided to borrow that one and take it home with me, but it's taken me until now to open it. I believe it's because I'm afraid of finding out the truth, that Wallace suffers from manic depression. If all of his symptoms and characteristics align with the ones listed in this book, there's no denying it. Of course I want to know what's going on with my boyfriend. But at the same time, confirming what he's suffering from makes it feel too real.

In the first chapter, the book lists the characteristics of a person experiencing a manic episode versus a depressive episode.

Manic episode:

- Lack of sleep
- Compulsive lying
- Manipulative
- Increased energy
- Increased agitation
- Increased confidence
- Poor decision making

Oh, God, this doesn't seem good. Does this mean he was in a manic episode when we first met? Everything listed describes the first months of our relationship. I'm in shock as I continue onto the characteristics of a depressive episode.

Depressive episode:

- Lack of motivation
- Increased sleep
- Feelings of hopelessness
- Lack of energy
- Loss of pleasure
- Weight loss or weight gain
- Feelings of guilt or shame
- Feelings of worthlessness

Wow. I stop reading as tears fill my eyes. I'm not in a position to diagnose, but these symptoms and characteristics describe exactly what Wallace is going through. He must have manic depression. At least now that I know the potential cause, I'll be able to help him get the correct treatment.

...

"I can't," Wallace says, sighing. He was able to get out of bed today. He's sitting on the couch in the living room. He hasn't eaten much in the last few days, so his weight loss is more apparent than ever.

"Why not, Wallace? You can't stay in this state forever. You need to get help." Why would he choose to suffer like this instead of getting the help he needs? I don't understand it.

"I can't be labelled as a freak. I refuse to be exposed like that," he says, avoiding eye contact.

Inside, I groan in frustration. I get that he doesn't want people to know he may have a psychiatric illness, but what other choice does he have? He can't keep rotting in the basement. He needs to be assessed by a psychiatrist, so he can be treated.

"You can't make me. If you won't accept me the way that I am, you can leave," he tells me. His voice is weak, like he barely has the stamina to say those few sentences.

His words hurt me. I've done nothing but be by his side since I found out he was struggling. I've done nothing but support him, and he's okay with losing me just like that? I try to remind myself that it's just the depression talking and not the true Wallace. In the books I read, I learned that those who experience depressive episodes will attempt to push away those they care about. I keep that in mind while I formulate a response.

"Fine. But you have to do something. Please, Wallace. I can't keep watching this depression swallow you whole. I need you. I want us to go back to having fun like we used to." I break into tears. I know he hates seeing me cry, but I can't help it.

He manages to put his hand on top of mine. "I promise, my Gem. I'm working on it. Every day, I feel a bit better, thanks to you. I'll be back to being myself before you know it." He gives me a weak smile. Then he tries to lift my hand to kiss it, but he fails. I put my hand in his and hold it up to his face. He kisses it, locking his gaze with mine. His dark eyes are filled with sorrow. I can tell he's trying to fight this. I just wish he would accept that he doesn't have to do it by himself.

Chapter 11

It's mid-April. The winter is behind us, and the semester is almost over. I only have a few weeks left before I officially finish my first year of uni.

Wallace is showing a lot of improvement. His energy levels are returning, and he's starting to eat more. Things are looking promising.

The last two months have been difficult. I've cried more during this short period of time than I have in my entire life. Watching the man I love lose his will to live has nearly destroyed me. After months of pleading for him to get help, he won't budge. Robin and Ramon have begged me to leave him. There's no way I can do that. Not only do I love him, how can I leave him during the worst time of his life? That would be cruel.

I speak to my mom about what I'm experiencing. She's the only one I feel like I can confide in. Robin doesn't want to listen to me. She thinks I'm crazy for sticking by a man who is "mentally unstable," as she put it. We had a big argument over it, and now there's been a wedge between us. We barely interact anymore. I don't want to spend time with someone who discriminates against those who are struggling with mental health. It makes me sad because my sister is my best friend. I never thought we would have differences that would ever break that bond. But I don't have a choice.

Ramon believes I deserve better than what Wallace can provide. However, he's a lot more empathetic than Robin is. He worries about me a lot. "He shouldn't be putting this burden on you," he told me. I was angry with him at first, but then I tried to see the situation from his point of view. He can't understand how impossible it is to leave the person you love the most while they're in a dark place. Ramon and I are still close, except we don't really talk about Wallace anymore. He understands that I don't want to talk about it, and I've realized that he'll never understand. My mom is the only person who fully supports my decision to stay by his side.

"It's not his fault, honey," she says while sitting across from me at the dining table. "He can't help that he's sick." She reaches out to rub my arm.

"I know, Mom. I just wish I could be the strength that he needs. I wish it wouldn't take so long for him to get back to being himself." I feel tears wanting to form. I'm not so sure who his true self really is anymore. After finding out about his mental illness, which part of him do I consider his true self? If anything, both sides of him are a part of who he is. I just need to accept that.

"He's a good man who comes from a good family," she says. "As his partner, you need to stand by his side and help him climb this mountain of sorrow. I'm not sure he can do it without you."

I agree with her. He's been incredibly dependent on me these last few months, and sometimes I feel like he can't live without me. I'm not one to give up easily, but it feels like I have so much weight on my shoulders.

"You've always been so strong, my darling," Mom says. "If God brought this man into your life, it's because you're capable of helping him."

I try not to chuckle at her advice. My mom is incredibly religious. She has a hard time giving advice without mentioning God's grace, but I still appreciate her words of support.

"Thank you, Mama. I love you."

She grips both of my hands. "I love you too, honey, so much. You and Wallace will get through this. I pray for you both every day."

Chapter 12

1989

I'm on Christmas break. It's December 31, and I can't believe I'm already halfway through my final year of school before becoming a teacher. I'm so excited. I can't wait to make a difference in so many children's lives. My dream job is about to become a reality, and I'm so proud of myself for making it this far, especially after all the obstacles I overcame over the last three years.

Wallace and I are still going strong. We just celebrated our three-year anniversary this fall. We moved in together about a year ago. Robin got herself a boyfriend, Norman, about a year before that, and she moved in with him about six months after they started dating. Wallace moved in with me shortly after.

I've been working part-time since I was sixteen, but with the current job I have as a teacher's aide, the pay didn't cover all of my monthly expenses after Robin moved out, so Wallace offered to split the rent with me. Wallace never returned to school after his depressive episode three years ago. Once he got better, he realized that teaching was no longer the career path he wanted to take. He was worried that if he got sick again, the school board wouldn't allow him to miss several weeks of work. He made the right move because he's had two depressive episodes since the first one. They didn't last as long, but he was still off work for several weeks both times. Luckily, he was able to find a job as a delivery driver with his cousin Jared's company. Jared knows about the family history, and he wanted to give Wallace a chance to make something of himself despite his sometimes debilitating mental illness. Jared has been understanding and lenient, but Wallace pays for it with his hourly wage. It's been three years, and Jared hasn't given Wallace a raise. Wallace doesn't complain, though. He's just grateful he can have a job and contribute to society even with the limitations caused by his illness.

We have a good system going. Life isn't easy, but I'm happy. Wallace makes me happy, and I make him happy. I'm looking forward to the life we'll continue to build together.

...

My parents decided to have a gathering at their house for New Year's Eve. I'm sitting at the vanity in our bedroom, getting ready for the evening. I got a perm done a few days ago, so it doesn't take long for me to do my hair. I often enjoy doing extravagant makeup looks for special occasions, but I decide to keep it a bit simpler for tonight. I put on shimmery baby-pink eyeshadow, mascara, concealer, and a touch of blush. It's my go-to routine. It allows me to have a nice glowing look without going over the top.

As I apply my favourite pink lip liner and lip gloss, Wallace walks into our room. "You look amazing, my beautiful Gem," he says. I give him a kiss on the cheek, leaving pink lip gloss on his face. He looks in the mirror and smirks. "You've marked your territory I see." I laugh.

While looking at us in the mirror, I can't help but think about how good we look together. It feels like it's meant to be. Yes, we go through our fair share of hardships, but our love is capable of overcoming it all.

"What are you wearing tonight?" he asks.

"A new dress. You'll see." I wink at him. I bought a brand-new tight-fitting pink sequin dress that I can't wait to show off.

"That's fine. I just hope the dress is pink. That's my favourite colour on you." He hugs me from behind. "And I can't wait until I can take it off," he whispers in my ear and then kisses my neck, giving me goosebumps.

...

Dan and Linda are here with the kids. Robin and Norman came as well. My mom insisted that Wallace bring his mother, sister, and brother. Just like every year, Greg is too busy to make it home for the holidays. I've always wondered how Greg is doing. Their mother, Rhea, always talks about how proud she is of Greg. She talks about how successful he is with his cleaning business down in Winnipeg. I don't know why, but part of me doesn't believe everything she says about Greg. If it's true that he has the same psychiatric illness as Wallace, how is he able to run a business when he gets depressed? Maybe he gathered the courage to seek treatment. That's something I still hope for Wallace every day. I feel like it's the only thing holding us back.

Dan approaches me near the snack table. He grabs a couple of egg salad sandwiches and puts them on a paper plate. "It's so nice to see you, Gen." He smiles at me before taking a bite of a sandwich. "You too, Dan. I miss you, Linda, and the kids. I'm sorry I haven't visited much. School has been pretty hectic these last few months." Dan doesn't know about Wallace's condition. I pleaded to my parents and Robin not to tell him. After what he went through with Greg, I know he won't approve of my relationship with Wallace. I only see Dan a few times a year, so it's easy enough to hide this information from him.

"It's all good, Gen. I completely understand. I wanted to tell you, I'm so proud of you. Our baby sister, just a few months shy of graduating from uni. You're going to make an amazing teacher." He kisses me on the cheek. I smile, tears of joy forming in my eyes.

"Thank you so much, Dan, I appreciate the support." I give him a hug. I can't help but feel guilty as I take in his kind words. I don't know how proud he would be of me if he found out I've been hiding something from him for the past three years.

"I believe that deserves a toast!" Wallace announces as he approaches us. He hands me a glass of champagne. Everyone else raises their glasses. "To my Gem. I'm so incredibly proud of you. I love you more than words can describe. Thank you for being my rock, my best friend, and most importantly, the love of my life." Everyone cheers as he pulls me close and kisses me. I kiss him back, passionately, not caring that we're surrounded by our family members.

"Now, let's dance!" My dad yells, trying to take the attention off of us. He turns up the stereo, and loud upbeat music fills the room.

Chapter 13

Everyone is dancing in the living room. My parents are dancing together in a corner, both of them feeling tipsy. They don't drink often, but when they do, they make the most of it. Dan and Linda are dancing with Robin and the kids. Wallace is slow dancing with his mom, even though it's a fast-paced song. Watching everyone having fun puts a smile on my face. It's not often that we have the chance to enjoy such a gathering. Everyone is so busy, which makes it hard to plan anything. Luckily, we're able to do this at least once a year.

Candace comes out of the kitchen with a glass of wine and stands beside me. She's wearing a maroon dress with fringes, and her light blonde hair is held up by a sparkly hair clip. Her heels are about four inches tall, but she's still slightly shorter than me.

"You look great tonight, Candace," I say.

She smiles. "Thank you. So do you, Genevieve. That colour is beautiful on you." She points at my dress. She appears to be in a pleasant mood. "I wanted to thank you for being there for Wallace. Before you came along, I didn't think he stood a chance against his illness. You've changed his life." She smiles at me in gratitude. "You have no idea how much you mean to him. He's so beyond in love with you. You complete him. I'm so glad you're in his life."

Her words mean a lot to me. It has been difficult earning the approval of the Browne family. Rhea doesn't seem to like me very much, and Candace was cold when we first met. It's taken years for her to show affection toward me. And Greg, well, I still haven't met him. I find it odd that he hasn't visited in three years, but I try not to pry. Maybe there's a reason he avoids coming home, and that reason is none of my business.

"Thank you for saying that, Candace. Wallace is special to me. I hope he sees that."

"Trust me, he does." She smiles and squeezes my shoulder.

"What are you two lovely ladies talking about?" Wallace says as he approaches us, taking my hand in his.

"Oh nothing. Just talking about how much Gen adores you," Candace replies.

"Oh well, by all means, continue," he says with a giddy smile. His eyes lock with mine as he grabs my waist.

"I adore you," I reply, wrapping my arms around his neck.

"I adore you more, my Gem. Now, please, let's dance. I want to see you move in that gorgeous dress," he says as he twirls me around.

...

As the clock approaches midnight, Wallace and I are the only ones still dancing. My head is lying on his chest as he caresses the back of it with his hand. We're moving slowly, stepping back and forth. Wallace is following my lead, not realizing that I'm moving us to the rhythm of his heart. I could stay like this forever. Such moments make all the heartache worth it. I'll go through anything life puts us through if it means I'll have this man by my side.

Our sweet, intimate moment is interrupted when Dan turns off the music. He gathers everyone in the living room to prepare for the countdown. He turns on the TV, where the news channel is broadcasting the New York ball drop. Excitement fills the room as the countdown starts.

"Ten, nine, eight, seven..."

Right before the last second, Wallace places himself in front of me, and everyone steps aside, leaving only us in the centre of the living room. The room is silent. He gets down on one knee and takes out a ring box. "My Gem, my beautiful, perfect baby." His voice trembles as tears fill his eyes. "Would you make me the luckiest man in the universe and marry me?"

My vision is blurred with tears, but I can still make out the perfect smile on Wallace's face. I answer without a second to spare. "Yes! Oh my God, of course! Yes! I love you!" I run into his arms and he swings me around as our families cheer.

"I love you so much, Gem," he whispers in my ear. Then he kisses me.

After he pulls out the gorgeous engagement ring and places it on my finger, he turns to our families and grins. "Happy New Year!"

Everyone cheers.

Chapter 14

1990

It's almost an hour after midnight, and I'm sitting on the couch, staring in astonishment at my ring. Wallace picked out the ring of my dreams. It has a beautiful solitaire diamond in the centre with a simple yellow gold band. It's elegant and timeless. It's perfect. I'm still in awe at what just occurred. I can't believe I'm going to marry Wallace Browne. I've been dreaming of this moment since our first date.

Wallace is surrounded by Dan, Robin, Norman, and his mother near the kitchen. Linda went to put the kids to bed, and she hasn't been back, which makes me think she fell asleep with them. Dad went to bed about five minutes after the announcement. He knew Wallace was going to propose, and it was the only reason he stayed up until midnight.

"I haven't seen the countdown in ten years!" he said before kissing me goodnight. "But it was worth staying up to see that look of pure joy on your beautiful face, my sweet, little baby girl."

My mom is a night owl, so she isn't showing any signs of slowing down. Whenever she hosts a gathering, she always rushes to clean everything up before the guests leave. Now that I think of it, it's probably her way of telling people to get the hell out. She has put away the leftover food and started doing the dishes. When I offer to help, she forces me to go sit down.

"You just got engaged! You're not going to clean up after everyone. Take the time to enjoy this beautiful moment. You can clean up when someone asks for your sister's hand in marriage."

Robin notices me sitting on the couch alone and decides to join me. "You're going to make the most beautiful bride, Gen," she says. She's wearing a gorgeous royal-blue dress that compliments her dark brown curls.

"Thank you so much, Robin," I reply, smiling. Robin and I haven't worked things out since we had that argument years ago. We've remained friendly, but things haven't been the same. I miss the friendship we used to have. There are so many times when I wish I could call her for advice or simply to vent. Yes, I have my mother, but there are certain things I want to share with my sister.

"Can I say something to you, Gen? Will you promise not to get upset with me?"

I hesitate and then nod. I don't want her to ruin this perfect night for me, but at the same time, I don't want to miss out on this chance to connect with her.

"I'm being honest when I tell you that I'm happy for you, Gen. But as your big sister, I can't keep quiet about some concerns I have regarding Wallace. I can see how much you both love each other, but I want to make sure you're thinking this through. It's one thing for you to help him through his mania and depressions, but how will that affect the children you may bring into this world? I'm aware of how strong and courageous you are, Gen. You've been that way since we were kids. It was as if you were strong like steel, and I was fragile like glass. I always admired you because you were always the one to pick up the pieces whenever I felt shattered."

By then, tears are streaming down her face. I'm crying too, as her words weigh on my heart.

"But one thing I know for sure, Gen, is that even steel can bend. You have the choice to make a change in your life, to ensure that you don't bend."

I try to compose myself, so no one else notices how much I'm crying. "Thank you so much for saying that, Robin. I feel like I've been waiting to have a conversation like this with you for years. I never brought it up because I was afraid you were going to judge me for continuing to love him despite how difficult it is. To be honest with you, I've thought about the future a lot recently. I can't imagine bringing children into this world without Wallace seeking help. There's no way I would expose them to one of his episodes. Children need stability, and Wallace is in no position to provide that for a child." It's the first time I've admitted those feelings out loud.

Tears fill my eyes again, and Robin hugs me as I sob on her shoulder. She lets me cry, then she holds my face in her hands. Her cheeks are stained with tears as her light green eyes stare into mine. "Gen, you have loved him unconditionally this entire time. The reality is, having conditions on your love wouldn't mean you love him any less. Otherwise, you'd just be enabling him, allowing him to succumb to his illness. You need to do this not only for you but also for him. If he loves you and cares for you, he'll make an effort to change. You may love him, but no love is worth this kind of sacrifice. Please remember your worth, Gen. He needs to remember it too. He shouldn't want the woman he loves to go through this much pain."

Her words sting, but I couldn't be angry with her even if I tried because I know she's right. Wallace and I can't go on like this. If he's serious about wanting to marry me, he has to accept the help that he needs.

"I love you so much, Robin. You're the best sister ever. Thank you for being there for me despite the fact that we've drifted apart these last few years. I never should've allowed for that to happen." I hug her.

"I should be the one apologizing to you, Gen," she replied. "I never should've attacked your relationship the way that I did. I have strong opinions, and I can be stubborn and even insensitive at times. You never treated me that way when I was with Rodney. Despite your objections, you always showed compassion and respect. I owed the same to you, and I failed. For that, I'm sorry, and I'm determined to make up for it. No matter the outcome, I'll be here for you. Always."

Chapter 15

"Can you believe four years of uni are already over?" Ramon asks with excitement. We have just put on our caps and gowns and are preparing to make our way to our assigned seats.

"No, I can't," I reply. This day is filled with emotions. I feel like so much has happened in the last four years. I look down at my ring finger and smile at the thought that I'm about to get married in less than two months. I'm equally excited to be done with school. My first teaching job is just months away! I can't believe I was able to pull it off.

"I know we won't be sitting together because our degrees are in different departments," Ramon says, "so I'll make this quick. I'm so incredibly proud of you, Gen. You've gone through so much over the last four years, and you still came out on top. I wouldn't have survived uni without you, and I'm so happy we get to experience the end of such an important chapter together." Ramon smiles at me, tears forming in his eyes. I reach out to give him a hug. He hugs me back.

"I love you, Ramon. You're my best friend, and I'm so proud of you too. But I'm also so mad at you for deciding to move across the country after graduation. There are plenty of software engineering opportunities near Toronto! You didn't have to accept a job that's nearly forty hours away!" I say it jokingly, but I'm sad he's leaving. Ramon has been there for me for the last eight years of my life, and I'm going to miss having him by my side.

He takes my hand. "I know, Gen. I'm so sorry, but I couldn't pass up a job offer in Vancouver. It's Vancouver, Gen! I've always dreamed of living out West. Besides, you know I'll be back eventually. I can't go too long without seeing you." He squeezes my hand. "Whenever you need me, I'm just a phone call away."

I smile, trying to mask the sadness in my heart. But I'm happy he gets to live out his dream. We hug once again before we start walking toward the auditorium, where the ceremony is about to take place. "I'll see you later." He winks at me and grins. We part ways as we head to our reserved sections.

...

My parents, Robin, Dan, and Wallace are supposed to show up at the ceremony, but so far only Robin and my parents have arrived. The ceremony is set to start in about ten minutes, and I'm getting worried. Where are Wallace and Dan? So many people are filling the auditorium. I warned Wallace to arrive early, so he won't be caught in the swarm of people trying to find their seats. He told me he was going to get off early from his day shift today, so he can be here on time. He's usually timely, so I'm surprised he's not here already. Then I realize this only happens with him when things start getting bad. When the depression starts to creep in, he seems to lose track of time. I've been so busy with finishing my placement, wedding planning, and getting ready for graduation that I haven't had the chance to see him much over the last two weeks. Due to our schedules, I almost always finish school or work when he starts his evening shift. When he finishes work after midnight, I'm often already asleep. Whenever an episode begins, his mood starts changing so subtly, it's hard to tell that something is wrong, especially when I'm not spending much time with him as I usually do.

As the auditorium continues to fill with people, I become worried. Something is wrong with Wallace. I look at my watch. It's already 1:52 p.m. The ceremony is set to start at 2:00. He's definitely not coming.

Dan finally arrives and takes a seat next to my mom. Wallace's spot appears to be the only one that's empty.

All the graduates are seated in front of the stage. Four different academic programs are part of the ceremony. I look for Ramon in the crowd of students in their caps and gowns. I know he's relatively close because I saw him taking a seat not too far from me. His eyes finally meet mine.

"Wallace isn't here!" I mouth to him, pointing to the empty chair behind us, where my family members are seated. I realize he's struggling to read my lips because he's narrowing his eyebrows and squinting. Finally, he gets up and comes over to me.

"What's wrong, Gen?" he asks as he crouches in front of me. "You're shaking."

I look down at my trembling hands, trying not to cry. "It's Wallace. He's not here. I have a bad feeling. I think he's feeling depressed again. It's been six months since the last time, so it's the right timing. I've been so busy lately that I didn't even realize his mood might've started declining. I feel like I'm such a horrible partner. How did I let this go unnoticed again?" My heart is pounding, and I have a hard time catching my breath. With all the commotion going on around us, I can barely think straight.

"Gen! Look at me. You need to breathe." Ramon takes my hand in his and rubs his thumb in circles into my palm. "I know you're worried about Wallace, but I'm sure he's fine. This isn't his first time going through this. And don't you dare blame yourself. You're only one person. You can't be there for him for every second of every day. It's not your responsibility to make sure he doesn't fall behind. He's the one who's refusing to seek help. He needs to accept that he can't put this burden onto you. He needs to take responsibility for his choices. You can support him and love him, but you don't need to fix him. That's not your role."

I nod, gasping for air while trying not to cry. Ramon lifts my chin and wipes the tears off my cheeks with his thumbs. "I know you love him, Gen, and that's okay. But ruining this moment for yourself won't help anyone. You've worked so hard to get here. You deserve to take an hour or two for yourself. You can go see him after the ceremony to make sure he's okay."

He gives me a weak smile. When I notice the look of pity on his face, something in me awakens. I'm not the kind of person who needs to be pitied. How did it come to this? How did I become a person that people feel sorry for?

I take a deep breath to compose myself. "You're right, Ramon. I'm not the one to blame." My conversation with Robin on the night of my engagement comes to mind. I've been avoiding having this difficult conversation with Wallace ever since that night. So far, I've had the excuse of focusing on school and being busy with planning for the wedding, but I can't go on like this. I have to make a change, or there could be devastating consequences. I have to give him an ultimatum tonight, or this cycle may never end.

"I didn't work my ass off these last four years to be crying on graduation day," I say, laughing while fixing my hair. I look down at Ramon, who is still crouching in front of me. "How do I look?"

"Gorgeous as always, Gen." He stands up and hugs me. After pulling away, he gives me a kiss on the cheek that lingers longer than usual.

"I love you," I mouth to him as he heads back to his seat.

"I love you more," he mouths back.

The ceremony finally starts. The teachers' college program is set to be announced right after software engineering. I'm so proud of everything Ramon has accomplished. His mother passed away from heart failure while he was in the second year of his degree. He took a few months off to work and to help his father with the estate settlement. His mother took care of the family finances, so his father felt completely lost after her death. He did everything he could to help him. Ramon's been taking care of him ever since. His father is still having a hard time coping with the passing of his wife.

Despite these new responsibilities, Ramon has excelled in his program. He was always a smart kid in high school, but he has made a name for himself in uni. Software engineering is hard enough, but he was also tutoring students, he was heavily involved in the program's research department, and he helped lead a study that is regarded as revolutionary in the world of computer science. Every time we hung out together between classes, I was in awe of how knowledgeable he was. I know he's going to do great things.

When his name is announced, I cheer along with his classmates. As he walks up to the stage to retrieve his diploma, he looks at me through the crowd and smiles.

"We did it," I mouth to him.

After accepting his diploma from the director of the computer science faculty, he throws his fist in the air. "We did it!" he yells, and everyone cheers.

Chapter 16

After the ceremony, we stay on campus for about half an hour, taking pictures with our families and reminiscing about the last four years. My parents have taken about a hundred pictures of me and Ramon. I can't imagine how long it will take to develop all of them.

"I'm so proud of you, honey," my mother says. I squeeze her hand to show my affection.

"I can't believe my baby girl is a university graduate!" my dad says, swelling with pride. "You're the first in the entire family line!"

"I couldn't have done it without your support," I say to both of them. For the last four years, they encouraged me to keep going, regardless of how difficult it was. They advocated for me through the negative comments from relatives, and they supported me despite their dated views on the role a woman should have in a household. They've done a great job of opening their minds to modern ideologies, and that's one of the many reasons why I love them.

My mother pulls me aside while my father speaks to Ramon about how he's going to need his help to turn on the computer he intends to buy in about ten years. "You know you've accomplished my dream," she says.

I give her a curious look. "What do you mean?"

"I never continued school after the eighth grade," she says. "That was the standard when I was growing up. Girls were discouraged from pursuing an education. We were taught to hurry up and find a husband, so God could bless us with as many children as possible during our childbearing years. I was blessed with three beautiful children, and I'm grateful. I'm not telling you this because I regret staying at home to take care of you. You kids are my entire life, and I'm beyond fulfilled." She gives me a look as if she's worried she might have offended me.

"I know, Mom," I reply, smiling.

"All I'm saying is that if this were a different life, and if I had been born in a time where women have the opportunities they do today, I would have wanted to do the same as you. I've always wanted to teach. Having a career, especially one that's so special, makes you feel valued. There's so much value in raising children and taking care of a home, but society doesn't see it that way. The fact that you pursued the career that I wanted but never got the chance to have, well, it feels like I finally get to live out my dream through you." Her eyes glisten with tears. "Thank you for giving me that."

I'm at a loss for words, in awe of this incredible woman. "It's an honour for me to realize your dream, Mom. I'll do my best to make you proud."

"You've already made me proud beyond my imagination, sweetheart. You'll be an absolute gift to your students." She hugs me, and I feel all of the love that she has for me through her embrace.

...

I arrive at our apartment shortly after 6:00 p.m. Wallace's car is in the driveway, so I know he's home. The odds that he's near the peak of another depressive episode are high. My heart is racing. The idea of having to experience this again is devastating, but I'm hoping it's the last time. I'm determined to get him the help that he needs. He can't continue to live this way.

Apart from his periodic depression, his manic episodes are also intense. When they peak, he becomes restless, his mind runs at a thousand miles per hour, and he makes impulsive, reckless decisions. He becomes a danger to himself and others. He puts himself in difficult situations that cause so many problems, and then he falls into a depression because he can no longer overcome those obstacles. The high and low periods usually happen within a year. Having his mood and behaviour change so drastically in a short time can't be healthy for his mind or body.

After I found out about his illness, he promised I would never have to deal with the consequences of his actions, whether from a manic or a depressive episode. He would often try to control his behaviour around me, until it became too difficult to do so. He kept his promise in a way because I never felt the effects of the financial burden he put himself through over the last four years. He must have some sort of arrangement with his mother because I know he spends a lot of money at times, but not once has he asked me to pay off his debts. After learning about his tendency to spend beyond his means, I haven't allowed him to spend a lot of money on me. As for our household, I've been controlling our finances to make sure nothing goes wrong. He's always been able to pay his share, so I've never had to question him.

Even so, I realize I've been ignoring the severity of his mental illness. Before Robin spoke to me about our relationship, it was as if I was in denial about the pressure I was under due to the instability that Wallace has brought into my life. We've been together for almost five years, and I've never had the courage to speak up about these issues. I've been afraid to hurt him or trigger the darkness. I've held on to those few months a year when Wallace seems like himself. As I get older, I realize that isn't enough, and I won't survive if we continue like this.

I enter the bedroom, expecting Wallace to be under the covers, consumed by sadness. However, he's not in our bed, and the room is untouched, exactly how I left it this morning. I start to panic. Our apartment is small, so it doesn't take me long to realize he isn't home. If his car is in the driveway, where could he be?

I call his mother, but there's no answer, so I call his friend Justin. He says he hasn't seen him. Finally, I call Candace. It rings twice. Someone answers, then hangs up right away. She's only a few blocks away, so I decide to drive to her house and see if Wallace is there. Candace has a small two-bedroom house that she acquired from a divorce settlement a couple of years ago. She lives alone.

I knock on the front door. I hear someone banging around inside, then she finally opens the door. "Genevieve! What are you doing here?" she asks, looking nervous.

"I'm trying to find Wallace. Is he here?"

"Y-yes, he is." She lowers her head, looking ashamed. "He begged me not to call you. He's going through a really hard time right now, and with the wedding coming up so soon, he didn't want you to worry. He was convinced that he would feel better if he took a few days off work. He came here so that you wouldn't see him in the state that he's in.

"He's barely slept in days. I was finally able to get him to calm down, and he's sleeping in the spare bedroom."

"How did he expect me not to find out? We live together! And how could he not realize I would be worried when he didn't show up at my graduation? When I saw that he wasn't home, I was so afraid that something bad had happened to him."

I grow agitated. I don't understand why Wallace would keep this from me. I know the wedding is coming up, but we need to prepare for this kind of thing. It's not like I haven't been through it with him before.

"Can I please come in?" I ask Candace. She looks behind her and then back at me, and suddenly, I get an uneasy feeling in my stomach.

"I don't think it's a good idea right now, Gen. He's overwhelmed, and maybe it's best if he stays with me for the night, since I have more experience with these types of situations."

I raise an eyebrow. How does she have more experience with these kinds of situations? Wallace told me that it was his mom who helped him through his first depression, which happened only a year before the one I first witnessed. After that, I was always the one to go through the stages with him as he recovered. I wonder if she's referring to Greg. Regardless, the fact that she's not letting me inside is making me suspicious.

"Candace, with all due respect, he's my fiancé. I've been through this three times with him. I've already seen him at his worst. Please, just let me in, so I can wait for him to wake up."

Suddenly, we hear a crash from inside the house. "Wallace?" I yell. Without a second thought, I run past Candace and make my way up the stairs, where I'm hoping the bedroom is. Once I'm up there, I hear a faucet running. Wallace is in the bathroom.

"Wallace? Babe? Open up. It's Gem." I try to keep my growing panic from my voice. He doesn't answer. "Baby! Open this door, now!"

Candace followed me up the stairs and is standing behind me as I unlock the door with a bobby pin, just like I did the first time this happened.

I swing the door open to find a horrifying sight. "Oh my God, Wallace!" I scream. He's unconscious on the floor, both wrists slit open. There's blood all over the sink and the white marble floor, spewing from his self-inflicted wounds. A bloody razor blade is on the floor near his right hand.

My vision is blurred from the tears streaming down my face, but I try to stay calm. It's the only way I might be able to save him.

"Candace, help me!" I cry as I approach Wallace. I cradle his head in my lap and elevate his arms, pinching the wound on his left wrist together to try to slow the bleeding. I'm able to feel his pulse at the same time. He's still alive, thank God.

Candace's hand is shaking as she hands a towel to me and uses the other to wrap around his right wrist. "Oh my God!" she exclaims. "How could he do this?"

"We need to stop the bleeding," I reply. "Did you call an ambu—" I'm interrupted by the sound of sirens coming up the street. Candace must've called them while getting the towels.

Moments later, the paramedics open the front door.

"We're up here!" I yell. The paramedics find us in the bathroom. They look stunned from the amount of blood that's splattered across the room. I feel like I'm going to be sick, but I'm holding back.

Minutes later as they take Wallace away in a stretcher, his face covered by an oxygen mask, the severity of what just happened sinks in, and I start hyperventilating. My throat feels sour, and I run to the toilet to throw up. Only when I'm done do I notice Wallace's blood all over my hands, arms, and chest.

"Go with him, Genevieve," Candace says. "Go make sure my brother makes it out alive."

I run downstairs and follow the paramedics. They allow me to ride along with Wallace. I hear them confirm a pulse, so I know he's still alive. I sigh in relief.

Once at the hospital, they get me to fill out some forms. One of the questions causes me to hesitate: "Does the patient have any history of mental illness or psychiatric disorders?"

I hesitate before checking the box for "yes."

Chapter 17

I pace around the waiting room for what feels like hours. The tragic events keep replaying in my mind. Rhea, Candace, and Robin are with me, waiting for the news on Wallace's condition. Robin knows he's been in a severe accident, but she doesn't know the details. Candace and Rhea asked me not to tell her, at least until they know what the next steps will be.

Wallace was admitted to the ICU. The only thing they told us was that he had lost a significant amount of blood and that he was in critical condition. Rhea hasn't shed a tear since she arrived. Candace has been whispering things in her ear, but I don't pay much attention to it.

"Take a seat, Gen," Robin says. "You've been pacing for almost an hour." I sit in the empty chair next to her. "When are you going to tell me what's going on?" she whispers.

"As soon as I can," I reply. "I promise."

I bend over and rest my elbows onto my thighs, burying my face in my hands. Robin brought me a pair of sweat-pants that she had in her car to change into, but my shirt is still soaked with Wallace's blood. I can't get the smell out of my nose. I don't understand how Wallace could do this. He's always been afraid of dying. He wouldn't willingly attempt to end his own life. There's something so strange about all of this. I try not to think about it too much because I'm afraid it will make me go crazy. I have to wait until I can confirm that he's okay, and then I'll investigate. There's no point in looking for answers right now.

"Did you have the talk with him?" Robin asks. She's probably wondering if a freak accident happened right after I told Wallace that if he doesn't get help, I won't marry him.

"No. I was planning on telling him tonight, after the ceremony. But when I came home, he wasn't there."

"Oh?"

"He was at Candace's house when the accident happened."

"Oh, wow."

"Yeah."

Finally, the doctor comes into the waiting room. She has a kind face and soft features. She looks to be in her early forties. "Miss Daley?" She looks in my direction. Wallace put me as his emergency contact when we moved in together. I was unaware of that, but apparently, he has made me his power of attorney as well. The nurses asked about it when he was admitted, and when I called Robin to tell her about what happened, she agreed to stop by my apartment before heading to the hospital to see if he had any documents there. She also thought to look in his car, and that's how she found the POA document. Wallace had left it in the glove compartment. He signed it a few days after we got engaged. It's as if he had anticipated that something like this would happen, and he wanted to make sure I was the one who could make medical decisions for him.

"I'm Dr. Aves, head attending physician of the intensive care unit. Could we please talk somewhere private?" I follow her into another room before Candace or Rhea have time to argue against it.

"What's going on?" I ask as soon as she closes the door.

"Wallace sustained severe blood loss. We were able to save him, but if you hadn't slowed down the bleeding when you did, he wouldn't have made it." I sigh in relief as she continues. "Due to the nature of his injuries, we had to put him on a seventy-two-hour psychiatric hold, and he'll have to be assessed by a psychiatrist before he can be released."

I'm so thankful to hear those words. After almost four years of trying, Wallace will finally get the help that he needs.

"I do want to mention, however, that soon after he regained consciousness, he was disoriented. This is normal, most likely due to blood loss. However, he was saying some things that were hard to understand without a proper context. We were hoping that you could help us clarify."

"Of course. What was he saying?"

"It was hard to make out, but he appeared to be saying, 'the candy made me do it' and 'the candy wanted me to succeed.' He repeated those two sentences over and over again, appearing distraught. Do you know what that means?"

I shake my head. I have no idea. "I'm sorry. I've never heard him say anything like that before. I don't know what that means."

"That's okay, Miss Daley. Sometimes, patients experience delirium after a bad physical or psychological trauma, so it's not unusual for them to say things that appear illogical. Once the psychiatrist makes his assessment, he'll be able to determine exactly what's going on." She gives me a reassuring smile.

"Also, when going through the forms you filled out, I see that you checked 'yes' in the section regarding his mental health history. He didn't have anything about this in his chart. Can you elaborate on that? It's important to know as much as possible, so we can ensure he receives the proper diagnosis and treatment, if needed."

I feel guilty for everything I'm about to tell her. I know Wallace has been afraid of learning the truth about what's wrong with him. He's afraid that once he's labelled with a diagnosis, people won't treat him the same way. However, he made me his POA, and there must be a reason for that. Maybe he set it up that way because, deep down, he knows he needs help.

For the next fifteen minutes or so, I tell the doctor everything I know. I talk about his episodes, about my research, all the characteristics I've noticed, and the symptoms he experiences. I also mention what Daniel told me about Greg. She does an excellent job at maintaining an even expression while writing everything down.

"Do you know if his brother ever sought treatment?" she asks.

"I have no idea. I've never met him. He moved to Winnipeg a few years ago and supposedly owns a successful business there, which is why he's too busy to come home to visit." She writes that down too.

"Interesting. Okay, so you're saying, to your knowledge, there's no family history of manic depression or other psychiatric disorders?"

"That's right. If any of his relatives suffered from mental illness, I doubt there would be a record of it. He and his family do everything in their power to hide it."

After a few more questions, Dr. Aves looks up at me. "He asked for you once he started feeling better. He told us he wanted to talk to you alone. When a patient is placed on a psychiatric hold, we usually don't allow family members to visit, in case it worsens their mental state. However, I think it would be beneficial for him to see you. What do you think?"

"Yes, I would love that. Thank you so much. Can I go see him now?"

"He's sleeping right now. We gave him a mild sedative to calm his nerves. I suggest giving him a night to fully rest. Tomorrow morning, you can come back, and we'll register you as a visitor in the psychiatric unit. A nurse will bring you to his room."

I agree that it's a good idea to wait until tomorrow, especially since my clothes are still covered with his blood.

She leads me back into the waiting area. I go straight to Robin and hug her. "He's going to be okay. He's been admitted to the psych unit. I'm going to visit him tomorrow because he's asleep right now. Can I sleep over at your place tonight? I don't want to spend the night alone."

She hugs me back. "Gen. I'm so sorry. Of course. We'll stop by your place first so you can shower and grab a change of clothes." She caresses my cheek with her palm.

"Thank you." I whisper.

Dr. Aves gives Rhea and Candace a brief explanation of what's going on. I can't find the strength to face Rhea or Candace, so I avoid looking in their direction as Robin and I leave.

We ride in silence back to my apartment. I can't stop thinking about what happened. I feel like I'm in shock. I hope this will be a wake-up call for him and his family. The severity of his condition is no longer something that can be downplayed.

"Are you going to be okay, Gen?" Robin asks.

"We'll see," is all I can say in reply.

Once Robin and I set foot into my apartment, I head straight to the bathroom while Robin waits for me in the living room. I rip my clothes off and jump in the shower. As the hot water flows over my skin, I try to wash away the trauma of the night, my body shaking with sobs.

Chapter 18

I wake up at around 6:00 a.m. the next morning. I barely slept all night. The image of Wallace unconscious and surrounded by a pool of his own blood on Candace's bathroom floor kept popping up whenever I closed my eyes. I may have had one hour of quality sleep at most. There's no worse feeling than waking up while something tragic is happening in your life. When you first open your eyes, you sense a profound feeling of uninterrupted bliss, right before the horror of reality sinks in. It all happens within seconds of waking up. The feeling of your heart dropping once you remember the pain of the tragedy is indescribable.

Since Robin and I both had a hard time falling asleep last night, we stayed up and talked about everything that happened before taking Wallace to the hospital. As painful as it was to relive it, I knew I had to tell Robin everything, especially since things felt off before I found Wallace in the bathroom.

"So, Candace told you he was sleeping when you arrived?" she asked.

"Yeah. She was about to tell me to leave when we heard Wallace fall to the floor upstairs."

"Wouldn't she have heard him come out of his room and go into the bathroom?" she asked. "He must've already been there when you arrived. Why would she lie about him being asleep? The whole thing seems weird."

"I know. Also, when I tried calling her house, she picked up the phone and then hung up right away. She must have known it was me calling. Why wouldn't she answer and tell me that Wallace was there with her? What could she be hiding?"

"That's messed up, Gen! What if she knew that Wallace was suicidal? Do you think she may have purposely let him slit his wrists?"

I didn't think there was any way Candace could do that. She loves her brother too much. Then I recalled what Dr. Aves told me. When Wallace woke up, she said he kept repeating "The candy made me do it. The candy wanted me to succeed." Was he trying to say "Candace"?

I shared what I was thinking with Robin, and her eyes widened in disbelief. "Oh my God, Gen, I think Candace was trying to get Wallace to kill himself!"

"We can't know for sure," I replied. "We won't be able to confirm anything until I speak to Wallace." However, from that moment, I was convinced that was what happened.

That must have been her plan all along, and I ruined it when I showed up. That would explain why she hung up the phone and tried to stop me from going inside her house.

She knew what Wallace was doing because she was the one who convinced him to do it.

The question is, why?

That's what I'm determined to find out.

I get out of Robin's bed and go into the bathroom to brush my teeth. Norman slept on the couch last night. I offered to take it instead, but he refused. He knows that I'm going through a hard time, so I appreciate the kind gesture. I don't think I would've been able to stay alone in the living room with my own thoughts all night.

I examine my face in the mirror. My eyes are red and puffy. It looks like I haven't slept in days. When I look at my reflection, I barely recognize the woman staring back at me. I look drained, hopeless, broken. I feel like I appear much older than twenty-three. The stress I've undergone in my short life is aging me.

I only packed some concealer when preparing to head back to Robin's place. I place a few drops on my finger and pat it under my eyes to try to hide the bags. Then I put my dark blonde hair in a bun and get dressed. After saying goodbye to Robin and Norman, I drive back to the hospital.

Once inside, I make my way to the front desk and ask the receptionist where I can find the psych unit. She points to the elevators on the left and tells me to go to the fifth floor and ask for a visitor's pass.

When I head up there, the doors are locked, and it's card access only. I find a security guard at the end of the hallway and ask how I can get in.

"Just a moment," he says after I give him my name. The short, muscular man says something into his radio that I can't quite make out. Then he directs me to a different entrance. "This way, ma'am, to the side entrance. Go straight to the third desk upon entering. A red-haired lady will help you with the visitor's pass."

"Thank you."

I walk through the large door, which is almost five inches thick. As I enter the hallway, I notice rooms with locked doors on both sides. The hallway is narrow, and everything is painted white. It feels lifeless and eerie.

After walking past about thirty rooms, I make it to the reception desk, where the red-haired nurse greets me. "Hi, Miss Daley. Dr. Aves told us to expect you this morning. Here's your visitor's pass."

The pass is basically a hospital bracelet. I assume they can't let anything potentially harmful enter the ward. She puts the bracelet on my left wrist, then orders me to take off all of my jewelry, including my watch. I hesitate when I take off my engagement ring, but then I place it in the bin.

"Don't worry," she says, smiling. "I'll make sure to keep it safe. Right this way."

I follow her down another hallway until we reach a door near the end. "His room is right here. When you enter, a security guard will close the door behind you and lock it. If you encounter any threat to you or Mr. Browne's safety, there's a panic button beside the door to your left that will alert the nurses and hospital staff. Once you're ready to leave the room, knock three times on the window, and the security guard will let you out."

The protocols seem extensive, but I understand why they're needed. I might think that Wallace isn't a threat to others, but until last night, I never thought he would be a threat to himself either.

As the security guard opens the heavy door, I take a deep breath and then walk inside. As expected, everything is white. There's a single bed, a small couch beside it, and a desk in the corner. The room is small, but it has a large window, which makes the room appear much bigger. Wallace is in bed, facing away from me. He's wearing a gray sweatshirt with matching sweatpants.

"Hi, baby," I say.

It takes him a few seconds to answer. "Hi, my Gem."

I approach the bed. He turns over and looks up at me. His face is pale, and his eyes are sunken. He doesn't smile, but I can see in his eyes that he's relieved to see me. I sit on the sofa next to his bed and take his hands in mine. I try to ignore the bandages on his wrists.

"What happened, Wallace?" I ask. I can't help the tears that want to escape.

"I felt like I couldn't do it anymore." He looks down, unable to face me. "I started feeling down about two months ago. Not long after our engagement party."

His family had thrown us an engagement party in March. I had noticed that he was slightly more sentimental around that time, but I didn't think much of it. I thought it was just due to the emotions involved with such a big milestone in our lives. However, he does become a lot more sensitive when he approaches the beginning stages of a depression. I should have noticed the change.

I was so caught up in the excitement, I failed to realize he was struggling again.

"I should have known," I say, my voice breaking as my tears fall onto our hands. I pull away from his grasp to wipe them off. He looks up at me.

"No, Gem. This isn't your fault. Please don't blame yourself." His voice trembles as he continues. "I'm the one who kept it hidden from you. I didn't want to ruin the excitement of our engagement or our wedding planning. I thought I could beat it on my own this time. I really did." His eyes water. I lean into him, and he holds me tight.

"There's nothing that's worth losing your life over, Wallace. You always tell yourself you can beat it. You have to be realistic, babe. You can't risk this happening again."

"I know."

I struggle to bring up what Robin and I discussed last night. Is it really the time for me to accuse his sister of allowing him to attempt suicide? I decide to ease into that conversation.

"Babe, I've seen you go through depression multiple times before, and it's never been this bad. Something's different this time. Are you hiding something from me?"

He takes a moment to answer, like he's trying to decide whether or not to tell me the truth. "The engagement ring, Gem. It's sort of what triggered the beginning of my depression."

My eyes widen. I have so many questions, but I wait for him to tell me more.

"I wanted to get you the ring of your dreams. When I went to the jeweller, I brought Candace with me to help pick it out. She picked the most beautiful ring I've ever seen. It was classy and timeless, just like you've always wanted. She told me that it was the kind of ring that would make you happy. With everything I put you through, I felt like you deserved to have something to represent how much you mean to me. I saved up about two thousand dollars to get you a ring. I've been planning to do this for a long time. However, the ring that Candace picked out was eight thousand dollars." He pauses and shakes his head. "Candace told me she would cover the difference as a wedding gift. I refused initially, but she insisted. She told me that she could afford it since her ex-husband had left her a lot of money after their divorce. Eventually, I accepted her offer."

"So, you felt bad about taking the money?" I ask, confused about how that would trigger his depression.

"No. I was grateful to her. It was the best thing she had ever done for me." He sighs. "Then the night of our engagement party, Candace asked me about the money she used to pay for the ring. She told me that she had gotten herself into some trouble and that she needed me to pay her back. Obviously, I didn't have five thousand dollars to give her. I asked Jared about picking up extra hours at the company, but he told me he didn't need the extra help and that he couldn't afford it. Candace was pressuring me to come up with the funds, but there was nothing I could do. Things started getting bad again, and I tried everything I could not to disappoint you. I couldn't ask my mother for that kind of cash since she's already done too much for me. I couldn't find it in me to tell you about it because I knew you would have offered to sell the ring, and I didn't want you to do that."

I was baffled by what he was telling me. I didn't know Candace could be so cruel. She had purposely set him up for failure. Fury brews inside me as he continues.

"The day of your graduation, she tried calling me multiple times after I got home from work. She told me to come over, saying it was urgent. Since I owed her so much money and felt so guilty, I decided to go. I figured I would make it back in time for the ceremony." Wallace's hands start shaking, and he struggles to continue.

"Babe, it's okay," I reassure him. "You can tell me. Nothing bad is going to happen."

"When I got there, nothing urgent was happening. Candace was just sitting on the couch, emotionless. So, I asked her what was going on."

"And?"

"And she told me that the only way I could repay her was by killing myself."

I am speechless. I cover my mouth with my hand to quiet my sobbing.

"I know it sounds ridiculous, Gem. But you don't know how bad my mental state was at that moment. I couldn't find a way out of it. I always experience suicidal thoughts when I am depressed, but I never act on them. I know not to go that far. But I was so desperate to free myself from this torment, from this pain, that Candace's words were the only confirmation I needed. I wanted to free myself from this lifelong burden. I especially wanted to free *you* from it. I felt that there was no other option."

He breaks down in sobs, turning his face away from me.

My heart shatters into a million pieces. I can't believe these thoughts were going through his head this entire time. I reach out and turn his face back toward me. "Wallace, how could you think that? I love you so much. You're the best thing that has ever happened to me. There have been times where things have gotten difficult, of course, but it's always been worth it. *You're* worth it, Wallace. Your death would have destroyed me." I kiss him on the lips and hold him. He continues crying on my shoulder.

"There's no way that Candace meant what she said, Wallace. There's just no way. Otherwise, she needs to be arrested. That should be considered as attempted murder." I say this to reassure him, but I have my doubts. After everything I've learned, there's no way I trust Candace. She is never going near him again.

"No, Gem. She didn't mean it. She was just angry. She didn't think I would actually go through with it. She used to tell me that if I made her angry when we were younger. I don't think she realized I'd take it literally. Please don't blame her. I'm responsible for my own actions."

He's trying to cover for her. Who tells someone with serious mental health issues to kill themselves? Especially after causing the depression in the first place? Unfortunately, without Wallace's support, there's no way I can prove what she did. However, it doesn't prevent me from seeking answers from her.

"I have no choice but to accept treatment. Otherwise, they won't let me leave," Wallace says as he lifts his head from my shoulder. I'm relieved to hear that.

"That's good, babe. I know you're scared. But this is what you need to live somewhat of a normal life."

He nods in agreement. "The psychiatrist saw me earlier this morning to do his first assessment. He emphasized how important it is for me to be here. I should have asked for help a long time ago."

"Maybe. But what counts is that you're here now. I'm so proud of you for accepting that you don't need to keep suffering like this."

He manages a small smile. "Do you still want to marry me?" he asks.

"If you promise to get better, absolutely."

"I promise. Whatever it takes," he says as his eyes glisten with tears.

Chapter 19

I leave the hospital at around 2:00 p.m. Before going home, I decide to stop by Candace's house. Before I have a chance to knock, the door swings open.

"What have you done, Candace? Are you fucking crazy? You tried to kill him!" I yell, clenching my fist.

She steps back, holding her hands up.

"It's not what you think, Genevieve! Please, just let me explain!"

"You told him to kill himself! You knew what he was doing to himself upstairs, and you chose to ignore it! You wanted him to die!"

"You don't understand! I couldn't bear to see him like that any longer! I couldn't watch him end up like Greg. I thought it was better for him to find peace just like our dad. I wanted him to escape this burden." She lets out a big sigh.

"What are you talking about? What do you mean 'like your dad'?"

"Our father had the same challenges as Wallace and Greg." She looks down. I refrain from speaking, so she elaborates. "He owned a cleaning business up until the late 1960s. Despite his mood changes, he was successful—for a while. Our father was good at pretending. He was so good that our mother had no idea he had gone bankrupt and lost his business until three months later. When he no longer had anything left to put food on the table, he went into the woods and shot himself. Our grandparents on our mother's side took all four of us in and supported us for years. Our mom was an only child, so she inherited everything they had once they passed."

She takes a moment to catch her breath. "She never admitted to us that something was wrong with Dad. She knew his behaviour wasn't normal, but she convinced herself that it wasn't real. When Greg started showing signs in his teenage years that he had the same problem, she reacted the same way as she did with our father and pretended that nothing was wrong. The only difference was this time she had the means to pay off any debts that Greg accumulated whenever he became impulsive. It didn't matter how much Mom helped him financially, though. There was always a trigger that caused Greg to fall back into a depressive state. It was an endless cycle, just like our father." She frowns. "By the time Wallace started showing similar signs, she had become completely numb to it. His actions barely got a reaction from her."

I can't even imagine what it must be like to grow up in a household with an unstable father and a mother in denial. Greg and Wallace were suffering from the same mental illness, and Candace had to witness all of it from a young age. It must have created a lot of unresolved trauma throughout the years.

"What happened to Greg? I thought Rhea said he was living a good life in Winnipeg."

Candace chuckles. "That's her way of hiding what really happened to him. He's not in Winnipeg. He's being involuntarily held at a psychiatric hospital in Toronto. He's been there for almost six years now."

I'm shocked by this revelation. Why didn't Wallace tell me?

"Wallace doesn't know, and that's why he never told you," she says as if she just read my mind. I didn't realize my facial expressions were so transparent.

"We didn't have the heart to tell him. Greg's mania turned into a hallucination-inducing psychosis. He started acting delusional, seeing people who weren't there. Hearing things when there was no sound. He became paranoid all the time. He constantly thought people were out to get him. He kept seeing the husband of the family he almost killed from his DUI incident a few years prior. He thought the man was following him everywhere, but it was all a hallucination.

"Eventually, Greg was placed into a psych ward after he almost killed a man who was walking down the street at night. Greg was convinced the man was the husband following him, so he stabbed him thirteen times with a pocket knife before realizing that he was just hallucinating. It was a miracle that the poor man survived being stabbed like that. After the incident, the court declared

Greg as mentally insane, and he's been locked up in that hospital ever since."

This revelation makes me so nauseous that I have to sit down. I wonder what the outcome would have been if Rhea had gotten Greg help instead of dismissing him. Hearing Greg's story makes me hurt for him. It also makes me sad for Candace. What she did to Wallace is horrible, but at least I understand why she did it. Watching her father and then her brother succumb to mental illness has had a serious effect on her own mental well-being.

"From the moment I met you, Genevieve, I saw how much light you had in you. To tell you the truth, I hated you for it. I wanted to find some light of my own, but I could never obtain it. I couldn't bear the thought of you possibly sharing the same fate as Wallace. I didn't want his darkness to overcome you. I figured this was the only way to relieve you both from the burden of this horrible disease."

"Candace, I came into your brother's life for a reason. He's the first person in your family to finally receive some help. This is his chance to heal." I look into her eyes, searching for a glimmer of hope, but all I get is a blank stare.

"I wish I could believe that, Genevieve, but I'm afraid it's already too late."

Chapter 20

July finally arrives. We've had a beautiful summer so far. The perfect weather for a wedding. The last two months have been filled with hope.

Wallace was officially diagnosed with manic depression. His psychiatrist started him on lithium a little over a month ago. Wallace kept himself on a voluntary hold until he started feeling better, staying in the psych unit for over two weeks.

I've already seen significant changes in his overall mood and behaviour. It took him a lot less time to overcome his depression, and he's almost back to a normal state. The doctor says it will take a few months for his mood to stabilize, but he's happy with the progress Wallace has made so far.

After Wallace got out, he wanted to see Candace. I went with him to make sure she didn't say anything bad to him. They spoke for hours about their childhood trauma.

It was healing for both of them. Wallace also forgave her for what she did.

During his recovery, I decided to pay the five thousand dollars that Wallace owed her. Even though she didn't want to accept it at first, I refused to keep the ring unless the money was repaid back to her. It was important for Wallace's recovery to have that burden removed, and I hated the thought of Candace paying for my ring. Paying it off also allowed me to let go of the trauma that was associated with it. It was my way of putting all of it behind me. I paid her a thousand dollars in cash that I had received as a pre-wedding gift from my parents. They had given me the money for my wedding dress. For the remaining three-ish thousand, I used a portion of the line of credit I got to pay for wedding expenses. I'm hoping we do more than just break even with the wedding gifts we anticipate receiving. We're having a fairly big wedding. We invited a hundred people, and if they give us at least forty dollars each, we'll make just enough to have our romantic honeymoon at Walmart.

...

I'm getting ready in my mother's room. She insisted that the bridal party get ready at her and my dad's house while the men get ready at Robin and Norman's place. I only have one bridesmaid—Linda, my brother's wife—and a maid of honour—Robin. Wallace has his friend, Justin, as his best man, and Jared as his groomsman.

We just finished getting our hair and makeup done. Linda and Dan paid for it as part of their wedding gift to Wallace and me. I'm wearing beautiful, shimmery, champagne-coloured eyeshadow and a rose-coloured lipstick. The makeup artist went all out. My face has never looked so glamourous.

My mother has been emotional all morning, and we still have three hours left until the wedding. The moment she saw me come out in my dress, she started bawling. "I've been dreaming of this day since I had my first girl. You look stunning, my honey," she says.

Robin paid for my dress as her wedding gift to me. I picked an elegant, minimalistic satin dress that hugs my curves in all the right places. I've never felt so beautiful.

My mother looks at Robin. "I definitely expected you to be in a white dress first!" she teases.

"Well, I won't be far behind." Robin stretches out her left arm and flashes her hand in my mother's face, revealing a stunning engagement ring. All four of us gasp.

"Oh, Robin, I'm so happy for you!" I say. "Congratulations!" I get up from my chair to hug her.

"Robin, that ring is absolutely beautiful!" Linda says. "Norman did an amazing job at picking it."

My mother cries tears of joy, gushing about how all of her children will soon be happily married.

When Linda asks about Norman picking out Robin's ring, I can't help but be reminded of the events tied to how my ring was chosen. I look down at my ring, sad that such a beautiful piece of jewelry is tied to such a traumatic experience.

Robin notices that my expression has changed. "I'm so sorry," she mouths to me. I smile back at her.

"It's okay," I whisper. "Don't worry."

It has to be okay.

When it's time to leave, a limousine pulls up outside the house.

"Surprise!" my dad yells as he gets out of it. "I know a guy," he says.

We all laugh, then I give him a hug. He takes a good look at me, tears in his eyes. "My beautiful, sweet baby girl getting married. That dress looks perfect on you. I can't even begin to tell you how much I love you. How proud I am of you, Genny. You are an absolute gift to that man. Please don't ever forget that."

A tear falls to my cheek. Robin pats it dry with a tissue. "Dad! Save the tear-jerking speeches until after the wedding!" she says. "You don't want to ruin her makeup!" She turns to me. "He's right, though." I smile at her. I have the best family in the world.

A short while later, we arrive at the church. It was my mom who wanted me to have a church wedding. "You need to complete the sacraments!" she argued. I'm not religious, but I love a church wedding. They're so beautiful.

Wallace is already inside with his side of the wedding party. My mom walks in with Robin and Linda. My dad reaches for my arm and interlocks it with his. He holds my hand like he's afraid to let go.

"Before we walk in there, baby girl, I want to tell you one thing," he says, his face serious.

"What is it, Dad?"

"If ever he doesn't treat you right, if ever he changes, promise me you'll leave him."

"Why would you say that?" I ask, puzzled.

"Because life is always full of surprises. I know you think your old man doesn't know what's going on in your life, and I may not know everything, but I know you and Wallace have been through some hard times. Now, I think he's a great guy, but that doesn't mean he always will be. Life, marriage, and children change people. So, I just want you to know that you should never feel stuck. You will always have a home to come back to, baby girl. As long as we're alive, your mom and I will take care of you."

My heart sinks in response to his declaration. I don't know why, but I feel a sense of relief after he tells me that. It's nice to have the reassurance that my parents will always be there to help me.

"I love you so much, Dad. You and Mom mean the world to me."

"We love you too, sweetheart. And like I said, we'll always be there for our baby." He kisses me on the cheek.

The doors to the vestibule open, and we walk down the aisle. I can see the look of Wallace's face from the other end of the church. He looks so happy, and he wipes his tears before they roll down his cheeks. My heart races. I've wanted to see that look on his face for a long time.

At the altar, my dad gives me one last hug and kiss before taking a seat. I look back at the crowd and see everyone I love—my family, Ramon, and the rest of our friends. Behind them are approximately eighty-five distant relatives who are basically just room fillers.

I turn back to Wallace. He looks so handsome. He's wearing a classic black-and-white tuxedo. He's gained some weight over the last few months, so he fills it out perfectly.

"You're breathtaking, my Gem." His eyes light up as he smiles at me and takes my hands in his. I'm so ready to become his wife.

Wallace is the first one to take his vows. "My Gem, the first time I ever called you that, it was an honest mistake. I could have sworn that's what your sister called you."

Everyone in the church laughs.

"After finding out I misheard, I held on to that nickname because I realized it fits you perfectly. You are a rare jewel. Gorgeous, valuable, and most of all, you shine in any room you enter."

My eyes start to water.

"You've changed the entire trajectory of my life, my sweet, beautiful Gem. I wouldn't be here if it wasn't for you. You've shown me compassion, you've shown me unconditional love, and you've shown me how to heal. Anything I accomplish in this world will be because of you. I vow to hold you dear to my heart forever, and I promise to love you through anything life throws at us. I'll be there for you until your last breath. You're my strength, my rock, my Gem. I love you more than you can know, Genevieve Daley."

Those are the most beautiful words I've ever heard. The entire church is sobbing. I'm a complete mess, certain that my mascara is running down my face.

After pulling myself together, I start with my vows. "Wow, I have no idea how I'm going to top that. I should have gone first." I laugh, my voice still shaky from crying. Everyone else laughs too.

"Wallace, I feel like I've been through lifetimes with you. From the moment you caught my eye, I knew you would become someone special in my life, and I've never been so right. We've laughed, we've cried, and we've hurt, but most importantly, we've loved so much. From the moment you placed that ring on my finger, I vowed to love you through anything that comes in our way. We stand here today, in front of all of our family and friends, ready to be forever linked. Seeing you today with pure joy in your eyes makes me feel like the luckiest girl in the world. I can't wait to make a beautiful and fulfilling life with you, Wallace Browne. I will continue to love you, uplift you, heal with you, and grow with you until our last breath. I love you so much."

Tears run down Wallace's face. "I love you," he mumbles before turning back to face the priest.

The priest says a few more words, but I'm too lost in the moment to pay attention. Wallace is staring at me with his mesmerizing gaze. He smiles while looking down at my lips. I know he can't wait to kiss me in front of all of our families and friends.

Then come the words we've been waiting for: "You may now kiss the bride."

Wallace takes me in his arms and does the classic sideways flip, pressing his lips against mine. We share a long, beautiful, passionate kiss, the first of many as Mr. and Mrs. Browne.

Chapter 21

The reception hall that we rented is big enough to fit about 150 people.

The theme for the venue is rosé champagne. The colour scheme is light pink with hints of gold. Rosé champagne bottles are placed at every table, along with champagne-coloured roses as accent pieces. My bridesmaid and maid of honour are wearing gorgeous floor-length gowns that fit the theme perfectly.

Wallace and I enter the hall shortly after the wedding ceremony. Our guests are already at their tables. When they see us enter, they get up and cheer for us. When we started planning the wedding, I was worried about inviting so many guests because I was afraid it would be too overwhelming. Weddings have doubled as a huge family reunion for as long as I can remember. I went to dozens of weddings growing up, and most of them were for distant relatives that I barely knew. Wallace and I had a big wedding mainly to make my mother happy. I was nervous since I couldn't think of anything worse than having a hundred people's eyes on me for an entire evening. Now that I'm living it, I realize it's not so bad, especially when I have the man I love most beside me, going through the same thing as I am. Plus, I know he loves the attention.

As I look around, taking everything in, my heart feels like it's glowing. I look at Wallace, or should I say, my husband, and he takes my hand.

"Are you ready?" he asks.

"Yes. We're going to have the best night ever."

We take a seat at the head table along with the rest of the wedding party. The first table on our left is where Ramon is seated with my mom and dad, Rhea, and Candace. With all of our family members, we didn't have room to invite some of my friends from uni. I would've only invited them for Ramon's sake, but he swore he was fine because he loves talking with my parents. He's been to my parents' house multiple times, especially in high school. They enjoy his company as well.

For dinner, we're serving a three-course meal. Our entrée is an amazing ricotta-stuffed pasta with rosé sauce. I may have gone overboard with making sure everything was on theme, but I will never get the chance to plan something this extravagant again. While Wallace was in recovery, I had to finalize everything alone, so I felt like I deserved to plan the wedding of my dreams.

After dinner, Wallace and I have our first dance, and it's so romantic. Afterwards, I have my father-daughter dance with my dad. It's beautiful and sentimental. So many moments from this day will stay with me forever.

As midnight approaches, most of our guests have gone home. Only a few of our more distant relatives are still on the dance floor. Rhea and Candace left at around 9:30, and Dan and Linda left a few minutes ago to put the kids to bed. Robin, Norman, Justin, Ramon, and my parents are still here. We're all tipsy, and we're having a wonderful time.

Wallace is probably the drunkest person in the room. He hasn't had a drink in many months, and I don't think he realized how low his tolerance is now. He's a happy kind of drunk, so it's not bothering anyone. He and Justin have been requesting 1980s rock music from the DJ for the last five songs, and they're drunkenly singing and dancing together on the dance floor.

I've been sitting at our table for the last ten minutes or so to catch my breath, and Ramon is seated with me. It's the first time we've had a chance to talk to each other all night. Ramon is leaving for Vancouver in two days. He was supposed to leave right after graduation, but he decided to stay for my wedding. I'm so grateful for his friendship. He's one of the few people who know me to my core. I'm going to miss him so much when he moves.

"The wedding was beautiful, Gen. Those vows were so touching. It was wonderful to see you glowing like that. I'm so happy you've found a man who treats you like the extraordinary person you are." His words warm my heart.

"That is so sweet, Ramon. Thank you! I'm so glad you decided to stay in town long enough to be here. I'm really happy you're here."

He smiles. "Of course. I wouldn't forgive myself if I missed my best friend's wedding."

A slow song comes on, and couples make their way onto the dance floor. Justin and Wallace are dancing arm in arm, barely able to hold themselves up. Ramon stands up and holds his hand out to me, grinning. "Would you like to dance?"

"I'd love to."

He leads me onto the dance floor. Then he puts one hand on my waist and holds my hand with the other. I put my free hand on his shoulder, and we dance to the rhythm of the music.

"I know I'm going far away for work, but I hope you know that, no matter what, I'm here for you," he says. "I know these last few years have been really difficult for you. I'm happy things have turned around and that you and Wallace are doing so well. However, if ever anything happens, regardless of what it is, please don't hesitate to reach out to me. I'll always support you and care for you, no matter how far away I am."

Throughout the years, I've told Ramon about everything that Wallace and I have been through. Besides Robin, he's the only person whom I trust. He's always there to listen to me and to provide sound advice without judgement when asked, and he has always supported every decision I've made. I know he worries for me and that he wants the best for me. That's why he's the best friend I could ever have.

"I know I can always count on you, Ramon. Thank you for being by my side from the moment we met. I'm incredibly grateful to have you in my life. I love you so much."

"I love you too, Genny. Always. I'll be home for Christmas, and I promise I'll make time to see you."

The song ends, and we share a long hug. The DJ announces that it was his last song and that he's packing up for the night.

"I have another small wedding gift for you." Ramon pulls a small envelope out of his jacket pocket and hands it to me. It contains two copies of the portrait that he took of me in ninth grade, the day we first met.

"I was going through my things to get ready for the move, and I found this in one of my old folders from high school. I didn't realize I still had them. I figured you'd want them to show your children one day and tell them about how good of a photographer I was." He laughs.

I take one of the photos, then hand the other one back. "Keep one. In case you forget my face."

"I could never forget your face, Gen," he says.

Just then Wallace stumbles between us. "There's my beautiful, gorgeous, wonderful, amazing, beautiful wife," he says, his words slurred. "Did I mention that you're beautiful?" He kissed my cheek, then he puts his arm around me and looks at Ramon. "Isn't she the best person to ever exist? God, I love her so much." He kisses me again. Ramon laughs.

"She's pretty great," he says, winking at me.

Ramon says goodbye to Wallace and me, then we share one last hug. Soon after that, everyone else says their goodbyes.

Robin and Norman have offered to drive Wallace and I back to our apartment.

"I love you so much, my handsome, amazing, wonderful, handsome husband," I say, playfully mocking what he told me earlier. "Is it time for us to call it a night?"

"Yes. But first let me drink ten bottles of water. I need to make sure I'm well enough to give you the best wedding night ever." He winks at me.

My face grows hot as I realize that Robin and Norman are listening. I thump him on the chest. "Wallace!"

"What?" he asks, a huge grin on his face.

He downs four water bottles on the way home, sobering up just enough to keep his promise.

Chapter 22

1995

Our five-year wedding anniversary is today. The years have flown past. Our lives have been busy but incredibly fulfilling. After the wedding, we made just enough money to pay off the loan I took out, and we had a bit of money left over for a weekend getaway in Niagara Falls for our honeymoon.

We spent the rest of the summer in anticipation of me getting my first teaching contract for September. I had gone for my interview with the school board in August, and they called me on September 5, the day before school, to offer me my first job. It was to cover an eighth-grade teacher's maternity leave.

The students I had that first year are why I still love what I do almost five years later. Especially over the last two years, I've grown confident and comfortable in my abilities as a teacher. I'm getting better at mastering different teaching styles to accommodate different learning abilities with my students. I've met all kinds of children since the beginning of my career. It's fascinating to see how every child has a life and a story of their own. I've seen so many different personalities, and every child is unique in their own way. Helping these children with the foundation they will need to grow into successful adults is so rewarding. I've already had a few children from my first year of teaching come back to see me once they've graduated from high school to thank me for the impact I've had on their lives. The sense of pride and joy I feel toward my students is incomparable.

Over the last five years, I've also learned that for some children, their teachers are the only stable adult figures in their lives. Some children are dealing with abuse or neglect at home, and they come to school yearning for love and stability. It's the most difficult thing to see as a teacher. It makes me want to save and adopt all of them, and being unable to do that is heartbreaking. The best thing I can do is support them and call social services when needed, but it's not always enough. That's why every day when I get to school, I make it my mission to acknowledge every child who enters my classroom. I'll never know if that small amount of attention they receive is the only thing helping them survive the day.

Teaching has helped me discover my love for children. Wallace and I have taken our time before having kids. We want to ensure we have good financial stability, and we also want to make sure that Wallace's mental health is doing well for a long time before we bring children into our lives.

Wallace has been doing well. He's been on medication for many years now without any complications. It only took a few months after the wedding before his mood stabilized. It was an adjustment for both of us at first, to live at such a normal pace, but him getting treatment was life-changing. There are no longer any setbacks due to his mental illness. We've been moving forward and building a beautiful life together, a life that we're finally ready to share with someone new.

I'm pregnant. I found out a few days ago when I started feeling different. I can't describe the feeling, but I knew something had changed. I took a test right away, and it came back positive. When I went to the clinic, they determined that I'm about six weeks along. I'm going to surprise Wallace with the news at our anniversary dinner tonight.

As I get ready in our room, my stomach is full of butterflies. I've been dreaming about being a mom since I was a little girl. I'm overjoyed that it's finally happening. I'm so excited to see Wallace's reaction. I know he's going to be an amazing father.

I decide to glam up a bit for our dinner, using colours similar to what I used for my wedding makeup, only softer. I have a stunning red dress that Linda gave me for my birthday last year, so I'm eager to finally wear it.

After I put on my pantyhose and slip on the dress, I look at myself in the mirror and caress my lower stomach. Knowing that my body is going to start changing in the next few weeks is exciting and terrifying. I can't wait to see my baby grow, but knowing that the body I've always known will never be the same feels bittersweet. I'm turning twenty-nine this year, and I've seen so much already, but somehow only now does it hit me that I'm a grown woman. It's hard to believe that, in just eight months, I'll be a mother, and that baby will become the centre of my life.

Wallace gets home from work at around 6:30 p.m. He works for Jared from 4:00 p.m. until midnight, Tuesday to Saturday. He's been picking up some day shifts every other weekend as well. Ever since he's started his medication, he's been keeping himself busy. He works whenever Jared can offer him extra shifts, helping his mother with her housework, and we've been volunteering together at the community centre a few days a week.

I'm currently on summer break, so I have time to visit my parents more frequently. Wallace takes a few weeks of holidays during the summer, so we can take a small trip somewhere. Since we're still paying off our student loans, and our salaries aren't high, we never do anything too extravagant. We usually take a road trip up north to go camping. His holidays start after today's shift. We have the next couple of weeks to celebrate the announcement I'm going to make at dinner.

We arrive at the restaurant, a beautiful steakhouse. Wallace wants to treat me to a fancy dinner to mark this five-year milestone.

"You look absolutely stunning, my Gem." He takes my hand and pulls out the chair, so I can take a seat at the table.

"Thank you, baby. You look gorgeous as well." He's wearing a white button-down shirt and formal charcoal-coloured pants. He sits across from me, looking at me with admiration. We've had our fair share of disagreements over the years, but he's never stopped making me feel special. He's always respectful toward me, even when we argue. He praises me and lifts me up when I feel insecure. His physical attraction toward me has shown no signs of slowing down. He still makes sure I always feel like the most beautiful woman in the room.

Before our waiter shows up to ask about drinks, I grab a gift box out of my bag. I set it up on the table in front of him.

"Gem, I thought we said we weren't going to do any gifts," he says.

We decided a few years ago not to buy each other gifts for special occasions. Since we're trying our best to save up, we felt that it was better to prioritize that instead of buying each other expensive things. Alternatively, we would just treat ourselves to dinner or write love letters to each other.

"This is an exception. Please, forgive me." I smile at him, full of excitement.

He opens the box to reveal a white baby onesie that says, "I love you, Daddy," a white pacifier, and the positive pregnancy test that I took a few days ago. The look on his face is priceless.

"You're pregnant?" he whispers.

My smile widens. "Yes. You're going to be a dad. The best dad."

He gets up and pulls me out of my chair, taking me into his arms. As he buries his face into my neck, I feel his tears trickling down my collarbone. He kisses me over and over again.

"Oh my God," he says when he finally releases me. "I'm going to be a father!"

He said it louder than he anticipated because he's surprised when everyone around us claps and cheers for us.

"I've been waiting for this moment for a long time, my Gem. I can't wait to see what our beautiful love has created," he says, kissing my hand.

After dinner, the waiter brings us a slice of chocolate mud cake with "Congratulations!" written on the plate in chocolate syrup. When it's time to pay, the waiter informs us that another customer paid for our meal to congratulate us on our pregnancy.

When we walk out the door, Wallace picks me up, full wedding style, and heads toward the car. We go back to our apartment that night and continue to celebrate.

Chapter 23

I'm now five months into my pregnancy. So far, the symptoms haven't been too bad. Fall has officially started, my favourite time of year. I love the crisp, cool weather and the colourful leaves. It's so beautiful. I'm back at work, and this year I have a permanent teaching position. I'm so excited to no longer have contract-based positions. Before getting a permanent position, I was never certain that I would have a job when September came around, which created a lot of financial uncertainty. When I was offered something permanent, I was ecstatic. I no longer needed to switch schools every year, and I could finally start to make a place for myself at my new school.

I'm teaching third grade this year, and my students are the sweetest kids you could ever meet. Ever since they found out about my pregnancy, they've been taking such good care of me. They make sure I don't stand up for too long, they bring me flowers and chocolates, and they are always offering to do tasks for me, like going to the printer or wiping the chalkboards. They are so precious, and I'm sad that I'm going to be leaving them in February for my maternity leave.

My loved ones were overjoyed when they found out about my pregnancy. My parents are excited. They check up on me twice as often as they did before, and they're always offering to help me with anything I need.

Robin has also been helping me with everything involved with the baby. She's gone shopping with me for cribs, strollers, and clothes and helped me set up the nursery in our spare bedroom. She's planning my baby shower, and she's so excited about it.

Wallace's family have been kind of absent since he announced the news to them. Rhea's reaction was slightly odd, and Candace didn't seem interested. I found that odd, especially since it's going to be Rhea's first grandchild, and Candace is going to be an aunt for the first time.

Ever since Wallace's suicide attempt five years ago, things haven't been the same between them. Even though Wallace and Candace worked out their issues, they continued to be distant with each other. Wallace also tried to speak with his mother about what happened, but she didn't care to hear him out. Instead, she acted as if nothing had happened to him. It makes me sad for him, to have a mother who was so cold and careless, even after he experienced such a traumatic, life-changing event. Wallace doesn't seem to be bothered by any of it, but I still ensure that my family and I give him as much love and support as possible to make up for the lack of it from his family. I understand that their reaction has to do with what happened to Greg, but I thought it would have been a relief for them that Wallace decided to seek treatment. Instead, it's as though they resent him for it. After what Candace told me about how Rhea reacted to what happened with Greg, I shouldn't be surprised that she was the same with Wallace. I suppose I expected her to act differently since Wallace came so close to actually killing himself.

To be honest, though, I'm grateful that Rhea and Candace haven't been involved in my pregnancy. I prefer to have a distant mother-in-law than an overbearing one. I'm happy I get to enjoy every stage of my pregnancy in peace, surrounded by my loved ones.

We've decided to wait to find out the sex of the baby. It's been driving Robin and my mother crazy. It does make it difficult to buy things for the nursery and clothes for the baby, but I think it's going to be worth it. I have a feeling it's a boy. Wallace is convinced it's a girl. Robin decided to throw my baby shower after I give birth, so people can buy things once we find out the sex.

Robin and Norman got married two years ago, and they recently bought a house. It's a beautiful home with lots of character, but it's a real fixer-upper. Norman works as a carpenter, so he's remodelling the entire house and adding an extension. The project is expected to take two to three years, and they want to finish everything before they have kids. In the meantime, Robin is excited to play the role of an aunt once again. She's growing more impatient each day in anticipation of my baby's arrival. I'm even more excited than she is, but I'm also incredibly terrified to give birth.

"I've done it three times. It's not that bad," my mom says to me.

She, Robin, and I are at a diner together for breakfast. I place my hand on my baby bump, which has grown quite a bit in the last few weeks. "That's not what you used to say, Mom. Please don't sugar coat it. I need to mentally prepare for the torture I'm going to endure in a few months."

She laughs. "Baby, just remember that no matter how painful it is, you know something natural is happening. And believe me, the reward is worth it. Besides, it's raising the child that's the most difficult part. Once you enter motherhood, you'll look back at the labour and think about how it was nothing compared to what happens afterwards."

I give her a horrified look.

Robin laughs. "Now, Mom, that's not very reassuring, is it?"

"I'm sorry. She said that she wanted to be prepared!" We all laugh, though I can't help feeling nervous. My mother notices.

"Don't worry, honey, it's nothing worse than what you've already been through. You'll be an amazing mother. I don't doubt that one bit."

"Thank you, Mama, I love you so much."

"I love you too, honey. More than anything."

Chapter 24

1996

I'm now thirty-eight weeks pregnant. I feel huge, I'm tired, and I'm always starving. My pregnancy has been relatively easy, except for these last few weeks. It's been a real struggle getting up and going to work every morning with how little sleep I get. Being this pregnant is so uncomfortable that I can't wait for the baby to come out. I don't even care at this point how much pain I'm going to endure while in labour. My maternity leave starts tomorrow, and I'm so excited to prepare everything for the baby's arrival.

Wallace is going to be taking a week off after I give birth. He's been acting anxious lately. He's worried about me giving birth, but I think that he's also nervous about becoming a father. He doesn't have a lot of experience around children, and he's shared his concerns about his ability to take care of a baby. I'm confident that he's going to be an amazing dad. He's responsible, caring, and loving. I know our child will become his entire world. He's been so protective of me ever since he found out that I'm pregnant, but it has intensified significantly in the last few weeks, especially when he noticed my discomfort. He's been an absolute dream at supporting me.

I'm in class and waiting for my students to arrive. It's late February, and there was a snowstorm last night. They announced on the radio this morning that the buses will be running late. I'm not worried because I don't have any lessons planned for the day.

My students have been working incredibly hard this year, and they deserve to have a little fun now and then. My class is already ahead from where we should be with their lessons, and it's going to work out well for my replacement. She'll have more than enough time to settle in and still be on track with everything.

Class starts at 8:15 a.m., but students don't start to arrive until around 8:20 a.m. I notice right away that five students are holding pastel-coloured gift bags as they enter the classroom. I tear up, knowing what they're for. I've always been someone who cries easily, but since this pregnancy, I cry over everything, no matter how big or small.

My students laugh when they see the tears in my eyes. They place the gift bags on my desk, and one student puts a sash around me that reads "Mommy to be."

Moments later, two of my closest colleagues, Victoria and Michael, come into my classroom with a cake, cupcakes, and other delicious treats. The cake reads "Congratulations Mrs. Browne! We will miss you!" in lavender-coloured icing. By then I'm a complete mess. I'm crying so much that I can barely get any words out.

"I can't believe you all planned this for me! Thank you so much." My students come around for a group hug. Afterwards, my coworkers hug me as well.

"You guys are the best. Thank you," I tell them as they pass me some tissues. My students' parents all came together to buy gifts for the baby. They bought diapers, onesies, and all sorts of plushies and toys. I can't get over how thoughtful it was for them to do this for me.

One student, Jack, approaches me after I finish opening the gifts. "Mrs. Browne, I'm really sorry that I wasn't able to buy anything for your baby. But I wanted to give you this. It's my favourite stuffy, and I think your baby would appreciate it more than me. I'm getting a little too old for stuffies anyway. His name is Fluffy." He hands me a little yellow duck plushie. Jack is one of our less fortunate students. His mother passed away from cancer last year, and his father was out of work for months afterwards, barely able to support Jack and his older brother. The school has donated food, clothes, and money to help them get back on their feet. Jack is the sweetest and most courageous child. It breaks my heart that he feels bad for being unable to afford a gift for the baby.

"Thank you so much, Jack," I say as I take the plushie from him. "I know my baby will love Fluffy. Are you sure you're okay with giving him away?" He nods with pride. I give him an extra-long hug.

"I love you Mrs. Browne. You're the best teacher I've ever had. I hope you'll come visit us with your baby."

"I love you kids so much. Don't worry, Jack, I'll definitely come visit with the baby." I smile, trying not to tear up again.

By then it's time for the kids to head out for recess. When I start to clean up, Victoria and Mike come to assist me. "Let us do that, Gen!" Victoria says. "We didn't throw you a mini baby shower, only to have you clean up afterwards! Sit down, pregnant lady!"

Michael and I laugh at her comment, then he helps me plop back down onto my chair. They clean everything up and then take a seat next to me. Vic and Mike are married. Victoria is a year older than me, and Michael is four years older than her. They met during Victoria's first year of teaching. She was lucky enough to secure a spot at this school after working only one contract, and Michael was already permanent here when she started. Her and Michael have been teaching sixth and seventh grade ever since. They tried having a child for over two years, but they recently found out that Victoria suffers from polycystic ovarian syndrome, which makes it highly unlikely that they can ever conceive. They were devastated by the news, but they are hopeful that they can adopt in the near future.

Despite their struggles, they've been so excited for me and my pregnancy. I've grown close to both of them since September. Wallace and I have gone on double dates with them quite a few times as well. Mike loves talking with Wallace, and Vic and I have so much in common. It's nice to have such wonderful coworkers. It makes me love my job even more. It also feels nice to have people in my life who don't know about everything that Wallace and I have gone through. Whenever we spend time with them, it's like we can forget about that part of our lives. It's nice that our new friends think that we're relatively normal.

"I can't believe it's been almost seven months since you arrived here for the first time and announced that you were already pregnant," Vic says. "I'm pretty sure it was the first thing you said to me! Seeing that look of joy and excitement on your face, I knew I had to be friends with someone who brought so much light into a room." Her words warm my heart.

"You both stood out to me on the first day," I reply. "You were the first colleagues I met who were as passionate about teaching as I am. I felt your positive energy from the moment I met you guys."

"We're so happy for you, Gen," Mike says. "We love that we can live this excitement through you." I can tell he means it, but I can't help but notice a glimmer of sadness in his eyes. I know that he and Vic are happy for me, but they must be constantly reminded of a child they will never know whenever the subject of pregnancy or birth is brought up.

Vic also notices her husband's expression change, and she caresses his cheek with her palm. "I know, baby," she says. "Whether it's from Mother Nature or the adoption agency, we'll have our miracle someday too."

I feel fortunate not to be struggling with infertility. Although they would never ask it of me, I remain mindful when I talk about my pregnancy. Of course, I can't pretend that I'm not pregnant, and knowing them, they would never want anyone to feel bad or act on edge because of what they're going through. However, I try not to brag about it too much. I can't even fathom how much it hurts them. Hearing of their struggles puts things in perspective. Michael and Victoria look like a happy, fulfilled couple, but deep down, this challenge that they are facing is hard on them. Victoria has opened up to me about how she hears Michael cry himself to sleep almost every night. Although he's been her strength through everything, he tends to downplay his feelings as a way of validating hers. He thinks that because she's the one who will never get the chance to carry a baby, his grief isn't as important. He's an only child, and as much as he won't admit it, Vic knows that he's disappointed that his family's bloodline will end with him. The reality is, it's equally difficult for the both of them, and I admire their courage. Through their hardships, their love continues to be strong. If anything, they feel even more connected now that they share this heartache. It reminds me of Wallace and I from before he started his medication. As difficult as it was to stay with him through everything, our love was unbreakable. His pain, his struggles, and his sorrow became mine as well.

"You'll both be amazing parents one day," I assure them. "The children who will get to know your love are going to be extremely lucky."

They look at each other and then back at me, their eyes glistening with tears. "Thank you, Gen," Victoria says. "We're so lucky to have you as a friend. We love you so much."

"Yes. And please let us visit your baby girl when she gets here," Michael says, smiling. He's been calling the baby a "she" ever since I told them I was pregnant. I'm just hoping that "she" shows up soon.

"I'll call you as soon as I can to let you know when you can visit," I reply.

They give me one last hug before our students come in from recess.

Chapter 25

I wake up in a cold sweat. I look beside me, and Wallace isn't in our bed. I look at the time, and it's just past 3:00 a.m. I feel a sharp pain in my lower abdomen that lasts about sixty seconds. Are my contractions starting? My due date isn't for another week and a half, but if my baby is coming now, I'm not going to complain.

"Wallace!" I yell. He doesn't answer. I struggle to get out of the bed, then I make my way to the bathroom to go pee. My mucus plug came out a few days ago. There's a strong possibility that it might be time and not just false labour. I waddle down the hallway, looking for Wallace.

Another contraction stops me in my tracks. I bend over and take a deep breath, holding my baby bump. I hear Wallace talking in the distance. It sounds like he's outside.

When I finally arrive at the kitchen, I notice the phone line stretched out to the door of the balcony. Wallace is pacing back and forth.

"What do you mean he's being released? I thought he was admitted for the rest of his life!" he yells. I can't help but wonder: is he talking about Greg?

Wallace found out the truth about Greg a few weeks after Wallace was admitted to the psychiatric unit. His psychiatrist thought it was important for Candace and Rhea to share that information with him, so he could understand how serious his mental illness can become if he continues to delay treatment. Rhea refused to be involved, but Candace agreed to tell him. He felt betrayed at first, but it made him realize that he didn't want to end up that way.

Wallace walks back inside and throws the phone to the floor. He looks angry and worried.

"Baby, what happened?" I ask, then I clutch my stomach due to another contraction.

His eyes widen. "You're in labour? Since when?"

"Don't worry, it's still early. The contractions are over ten minutes apart. My OBGYN told me that I only need to go to the hospital once my contractions are five minutes apart or less." I breathe heavily as he walks me to the sofa, so I can sit down.

"Who was that?" I ask. "And why did you throw the phone?" I'm anxious for answers to the hundreds of questions that are filling my head. I also need a distraction from worrying about the pain of my next contraction.

"It was Candace. She told me that Greg was reassessed recently, and his psychiatrist thinks he'll be ready for release in the next month or so." He sits next to me and places his forehead into his palms. "They told me there were no chances of that happening. I don't know how I feel about Greg being released at all, let alone so soon after the baby arrives."

I feel sick to my stomach, but I try to reassure him—and myself. "Wallace, you're living proof that recovery is possible. Maybe his treatment is working, and he's no longer a threat to himself or others. He's been admitted for a long time now. He deserves a second chance at a better life. Don't you think?"

He takes a moment to reflect, then nods in agreement. "You're right. I shouldn't be so quick to judge. He never had the support that I've been lucky enough to get from you. I could've easily ended up in the same situation as him."

As he kisses my forehead, I feel another contraction coming. They're about seven minutes apart now, and they seem to be lasting longer. The pain has also intensified.

"Are you okay?" he asks, putting a hand on my lower back. I try to steady my breathing, just like the maternity books have taught me. It's not really helping with the pain or the panic that I'm starting to feel inside.

"I don't know if I can go through this," I say, looking at him. "I'm scared."

"If anyone can go through this, it's you, my Gem. Please tell me how I can help."

The next contraction comes less than five minutes later. "You can help by bringing me to the hospital," I reply. "I think the baby is coming soon."

...

Even though the hospital is ten minutes away, it takes Wallace only five minutes to get there. He's so nervous, he's sweating like crazy.

It takes about twenty minutes for me to be admitted. When the doctor checks my cervix, she confirms that I'm already eight centimetres dilated. She also informs me that it's too late to get an epidural. I guess I have no choice but to go through with my plan to deliver naturally. The pain is so intense that I feel like I'm going to faint.

I'm sweating profusely, and it's a struggle to breathe. I tell Wallace to shut up and not to touch me; the pain is unbearable. Like the good husband that he is, he knows better than to argue, and he stands next to me in silence, respecting my wishes. I don't understand how women survive this. It's the worst pain I've ever felt.

After having intense contractions for over two hours, the nurse prepares me for delivery. I feel a lot of pressure down there, and I get a sudden urge to push. When I tell the nurse that, she nods in understanding.

"Okay, when your next contraction comes, I want you to push as hard as you can, Genevieve."

I look at Wallace, and he takes my hand. When I feel the contraction, I push with all of my strength.

I push for over an hour, without any luck. I've been trying so hard that I've fainted multiple times. The doctor says the baby is stuck in the birth canal, right under my pubic bone, and they need to use forceps.

"Won't that hurt the baby?" Wallace asks, his eyes full of panic.

"It's unlikely," my doctor replies. "However, keeping the baby in the birth canal any longer will cut off the oxygen supply. We need to act now to make sure there are no complications."

I read about this kind of scenario in one of my maternity books, so I know I can trust what the doctor is saying. I try to reassure Wallace by looking at him and nodding. He squeezes my hand.

"Okay, Genevieve, I'm going to count to three and then I want you to push with everything you have," my doctor says. "I'm hoping this will be the last time."

I brace myself as the contraction comes in full force. As I push, I feel the doctor place the forceps on the baby's head. A few seconds later, I hear a cry, and I'm overcome with relief.

"Congratulations! You have a beautiful baby girl."

The doctor helps Wallace cut the umbilical cord, then she places the baby on my chest. Tears run down my face as I place her little cheek next to mine. "Oh, baby girl. I'm so happy you're here." I kiss her little face.

Wallace looks starstruck beside me. He kisses my forehead. "You did it, my Gem. Isn't she the most precious little thing? I can't believe we made her."

The nurse takes her from me to clean her and weigh her, then she brings her right back, wrapped up in a blanket with a pink beanie on her head. She's the most beautiful baby I've ever seen. Her lips are full, and she has a full head of dark hair, just like her father.

"She looks just like you, Daddy," I say. "Here, hold her."

His eyes light up with admiration as he takes her from me, cradling her in his arms. "She's so tiny," he says. "I can't believe it." His eyes don't leave her for even a second.

The nurse confirms that she weighs six pounds and eleven ounces. She looks so fragile and petite. She grunts and squirms in her blanket, and Wallace tenses up.

"It's okay, babe," I assure him. "Babies do that. You're not hurting her."

He relaxes and rocks her gently. "I'm going to protect you, sweet girl. Always," he whispers.

"So, do you think she suits the baby name we picked out?" I ask.

He nods. "Absolutely. I think it's perfect."

"Welcome to the world, Alaina," I say, rubbing my thumb on her tiny cheek.

Chapter 26

The next few weeks fly by. Alaina will be a month old tomorrow. Our first month as parents hasn't been the easiest. Alaina cries a lot, and Wallace and I are sleep deprived. Over the past week, she's been feeding every two hours, and whenever she starts to cry, I want to cry with her. Postpartum recovery is difficult for me as well. I've never heard a new mother talk about how painful it is. I had second-degree tearing, and having to go to the bathroom was excruciating at first.

Another thing that I was surprised about were the contractions after I gave birth. They were especially strong when I was breastfeeding. Going through that pain after the trauma of labour and delivery was indescribable. I was thankful that Wallace took the week off after the birth to take care of the baby and me. I don't know what I would have done during that first week without him.

Once he returned to work, his schedule worked well for us to sleep in shifts. I stay up until about 1:00 a.m., and then he takes over from then until about 8:00 a.m. Afterwards, he sleeps until he has to get ready for work. It's tiring for the both of us, and we barely get to spend any time together, but we both know it's temporary, and it's the only way for us to survive this newborn stage. It also allows each of us to bond with Alaina. When the weekends come around, we appreciate the time we get to spend together.

During the day, my parents have been coming over to keep me company. My mom cooked meals for me and Wallace for two weeks straight, and she still brings us leftovers from the supper she made for her and Dad the night before.

Robin and Norman have come by a few times since Alaina was born, and I've invited Mike and Vic too. I had my baby shower last week, and it was a wonderful afternoon. All of my favourite ladies were in attendance. Linda and my nieces were there, and it was the first time they got to meet Alaina. Dan and all the other boys came by to crash the party toward the end.

Candace and Rhea weren't there. Robin invited them, but they didn't show. They haven't even met Alaina yet.

I know it bothers Wallace to see all the support from my family while we receive none from his. It makes me sad for him that his family is absent during the happiest time of his life.

After the conversation he had on the phone with Candace the night I went into labour, he avoids talking about her or his mother. Whenever I bring them up, he changes the topic. I asked him about Greg's release, but Wallace doesn't think it's going to happen. I try not to ask him about it too much, because I don't want to upset him.

...

I wake up and I look at the time. It's 2:20 a.m. Wallace isn't beside me, and the apartment is silent. Usually, I can hear Wallace moving around in the nursery through the baby monitor, or I hear the TV on in the living room. When Alaina is fussy, he tries to soothe her in the living room, so I can sleep. However, it's as if they aren't here at all.

I get up and go straight to the nursery. Alaina is in there, sleeping. I sigh in relief, thinking maybe Wallace fell asleep in the living room.

Sure enough, I find him asleep on the sofa. Then I do a double take. It's not Wallace; it's Candace!

"Candace! What are you doing here?" I ask, shaking her awake. "Where's Wallace?"

Candace's eyes open, and she looks around in confusion. Then her eyes widen when she sees me standing over her.

"Oh, Genevieve, Wallace told me you wouldn't wake up," she says, sounding disappointed. "You weren't supposed to find out."

"What the hell are you talking about?" I ask. "Where is he?"

"He went to see Greg. Greg was released a few nights ago, and he's staying with me. I offered to watch Alaina while he went to see him. He didn't want to worry you, and he made sure to leave right after Alaina's last feeding.

He told me that neither of you would wake up before he got back. I'm really sorry."

I don't understand why Wallace wouldn't wake me up to let me know. And why is he visiting Greg in the middle of the night? It's so strange. Most of all, I can't believe Wallace would leave Alaina under Candace's supervision, especially after what she tried doing to him. I feel betrayed and hurt but mostly worried. I'm afraid something will happen to Wallace. I have a horrible feeling in my stomach that won't go away.

"Candace, what were you thinking? Why would you let Wallace go see Greg in the middle of the night? Do you even know if Greg is safe to be around?"

I leave the living room before she has time to answer and call Robin to tell her I'm on my way over with Alaina. Without hesitation, she tells me that she and Norman will be waiting for me.

I go to the nursery and take Alaina in my arms. She's still sound asleep, so I carry her to our front entrance and place her into her carrier. Then I grab my diaper bag and three bottles out of the fridge, along with a large ice pack.

"What are you doing, Genevieve?"

"I'm bringing Alaina over to Robin's. There's no way that I'm leaving Wallace alone with Greg. You can either come with me or stay here until we get back. I don't care. But I'm leaving."

"I'm coming," she replies.

As we pull out of the driveway, I glance at Candace, who's staring at her hands as she fidgets in her seat.

"I know there's more to it than what you let on back in the apartment," I say. "You wouldn't agree to watch

Alaina unless it was something serious. You haven't even met her yet! You couldn't be bothered to come over after she was born."

"I'm sorry, Genevieve," she mutters.

"Are you?"

"Yes! My mother and I have stayed away because we figured it was for the best."

I wait for her to continue.

"Wallace called us the day she was born. He sounded so excited. I didn't want us to ruin his joy with the negativity our family brings into his life. He says he's moved past what happened, and he's forgiven us for keeping what happened to Greg a secret, but I know that, deep down, he resents us for it. He resents us for our lack of empathy toward our father when he died, and he especially resents me for setting him up to fail. And in all honesty, he's right to feel that way. I did fail him. I never should have believed that he was beyond redemption. I never should have been so cruel to him. So, I promised him that Mom and I would stay away from Alaina. We can't undo what we've already done to him, but we can at least try not to interfere with his children. We owe him that much."

I park in front of Robin's house and look into her eyes. "Do you feel bad for anything you and your mother put him through?"

"I wish I could say I do. But if I'm being completely honest, I feel detached from him. I've always done what I thought was best for Wallace, and I never considered how much of an impact it could have on him. Since we were kids, I've lied to him and manipulated him. I just assumed he wouldn't stand a chance, so in my mind, I made him into a villain. I ignored the part of him that was compassionate, kind, and loving, and I only saw his disease. That way I would never feel bad for all the things that I've done."

I sit in silence, pondering her words.

"There's something wrong with all of us," she says. "I accepted that a long time ago. I don't know if it's due to the trauma that we experienced or if it was our mother's lack of empathy and love that caused us to be this way, but we all have minds that turn against us. I take after our mother, and Greg and Wallace have become like our father. If Alaina or any of your other future children are to stand a chance, it's better if we're not a part of their lives."

"I'm sorry it's turned out this way," I reply. "I can't even imagine what you've all been through. However, if you want to help Wallace, I don't think that seeing Greg is what's best for him. We have no idea what that could trigger for him. You can't do something like this again without letting me know."

She nods in agreement. "I won't. I promise." She doesn't apologize, though.

Norman comes out and runs to the car. I get out and greet him while Candace stays in the car.

"What's going on?" he asks. "Robin said you sounded worried on the phone."

He takes the baby carrier from me and starts speed walking toward the house. I'm right behind him, ensuring that the blanket I placed over Alaina is keeping her from getting wet. It started pouring while we were driving.

As soon as we get inside, Robin hugs me. "What the hell is going on, Gen? Is Wallace in trouble?"

"I'm not sure. I promise I'll tell you everything as soon as I know. I need to get to Candace's house as quickly as possible. I'll come back and get Alaina as soon as I can."

"Be careful!" Robin yells as I run back to the car.

I speed toward Candace's house. As soon as we arrive, I run toward her front door without checking if she's following me. Thankfully, the door is unlocked.

"Wallace? Wallace, are you here? Please answer me!" I cry. It's completely silent.

"Greg? Where are you?" Candace calls out behind me. We look throughout the entire home, but neither of them are here.

"The back patio door is unlocked!" Candace announces.

Her backyard is near a large, wooded area, so they could be anywhere, miles away from us. I look back at Candace, trying to catch my breath.

"I have an idea where they might be," she says. "Follow me."

A few yards into the bushes, I notice a trail.

"It leads to an abandoned bridge from the old highway," Candace says. "I have a feeling they might be up there. It's maybe a kilometre or two away."

We run as fast as we can. About ten minutes later, we arrive at the abandoned bridge, spotting three silhouettes in the distance.

Who could be with them?

As soon as we reach the bridge, my mouth falls open. It takes a moment for what I'm seeing to register.

"Daniel? What are you doing here?" I say in utter shock. Dan hasn't seen Greg in years. Why the hell is he here with him and Wallace in the middle of the night?

"I'll explain later," he replies, signalling for me to stay where I am. His voice is trembling, and he looks terrified. All three of them look distraught, especially Greg.

Greg is different from how I imagined him. He doesn't look like Wallace at all. He has light hair and a tall, slim build. His eyes are sunken, and his face is pale and contorted with a panicked expression.

"No, no, no! Wallace, tell them to leave now!" he yells. He shakes his head and mumbles incoherently.

I look at Candace in horror, but she doesn't seem at all bothered by it, which makes me feel uneasy.

"Wallace, what's going on?" I shout as I move closer to him. The bridge is slippery from the rain and has a lot of cracked bricks. Some of them seem unstable, so I move forward with caution.

"Stop, Genevieve!" Wallace says. "It's too dangerous for you to be here! Candace, you were supposed to watch her! Where's Alaina? Please tell me she's not here." Wallace's hands are shaking, his eyes are bloodshot, and he stutters when he speaks.

"She's with Robin!" I tell him. "Don't worry. She's safe."

"And you should know there's no way I could have kept your wife from coming to find you!" Candace adds.

Before Wallace can respond, Greg grabs him by the collar. "I don't give a fuck if we have an audience. There's nothing they can do to stop me." He pulls Wallace closer to the edge of the bridge, then he looks back at us. "There's no way to stop it. No matter what you try, you'll always succumb to the darkness." Greg laughs hysterically. Tears stream down his face as he shakes his head.

Wallace tries to break his grip. "Greg. You have to listen to me. There's hope for recovery. I've been doing good for over six years!"

"You say that, Wallace. But I know there's still a small part of you that can't stand who you've become. There's always going to be a voice in that fucked-up head of yours telling you that feeling the euphoric high again is worth it. Our brains are programmed to surrender to temptation, and it's a struggle every single day."

Wallace winces as Greg screams in his face.

"There's no point in trying," Greg continues. "I've been in prison for years, and I'm not talking about that fucking hospital. I'm talking about in here!" He points to his head. "This fucking disease," he continues, gasping for air between sobs, "it'll end you. There's no escaping it. No matter how long you think you can resist the urge." He has a sinister look in his eyes as he stares at Wallace. "I'm ending this for both of us. I'm freeing us from this endless torture. It's not worth the fight."

I scream and try to run and stop him, but Candace pulls me back. "You can't, Genevieve!" she yells. "You can't risk leaving Alaina without a mother or a father!"

Just before Greg tries to pull Wallace off the bridge, Daniel grabs Wallace's arm to pull him out of Greg's grasp. All three of them fall forward, and Greg is left lying on his back by the edge of the bridge. Wallace and Dan get up and hold onto him, trying to keep him from jumping over the edge, but he breaks free and then heads toward Wallace. Daniel pushes Greg away from Wallace, and Greg loses his balance. He goes over the edge of the bridge, falling fifteen feet.

"Greg!" Wallace screams, his voice echoing off the nearby rocks. I run toward him and hold him as he collapses to the ground. Daniel puts his arms around both of us.

"I thought I could help him," Wallace says. "I wanted to show him that there was a way out." Wallace cries into his sleeve. "I should have been there for him."

"This isn't your fault Wallace," Daniel says. "There's nothing you could have done to help him. You didn't even know he was locked up." His attempt at assurance just makes Wallace cry harder.

I hear sirens in the distance. Candace disappeared a few minutes after Greg fell. She must have headed down the trail to direct the paramedics toward the bridge.

When the paramedics arrive, everyone is so shaken that they can barely speak. Greg's horrifying words play in my mind, along with the sound of his skull cracking as it hit the pavement below the bridge.

A small part of me worries that Greg might be right. What if there's no way for Wallace to escape his illness?

Chapter 27

Everyone is gathered at the hospital, and we're all seated in the waiting room. The doctors haven't come by to confirm whether Greg is going to make it. Robin and Norman arrived with Alaina. They ran out of bottles, and she needed to be fed again, so they brought her to me.

They're staying alongside Wallace and me. I'm still in shock. We have gone years without anything bad happening to us, and life was finally starting to feel normal.

Wallace hasn't spoken a word since we arrived, and he refuses to look at me. I'm worried about how this will affect him, especially if Greg doesn't make it.

Daniel stands up. "I'm going to get coffee. Does anyone else want some?"

No one answers, but Robin and I stand up too. "We can come with you," she says.

Dan grabs Alaina's carrier for me, then starts walking. Robin and I follow. She's been waiting all night to find out what happened, and I've been wanting to pull Dan aside to find out why he was on the bridge with Greg and Wallace.

We stop in front of the coffee machine at the end of the hallway.

"Dan, why were you with them?" I ask. "Why didn't you call me?"

"I didn't have time," he replies. "Wallace wasn't supposed to be there. He arrived at Candace's house shortly after me. I had no idea that Greg had reached out to him too.

"I got a call from Greg at midnight, just before I was about to go to bed. He wasn't making sense, and he sounded deranged. I assume he found my number in the phone book.

"He said he needed me and that I was the only person who could stop him from hurting himself. I wasn't sure how serious he was, so I offered to meet him where he was staying. I didn't know he had just gotten out of the hospital. Before tonight, all I knew was what I told you about him all those years ago. I had no idea that he got locked up for stabbing someone. Even though we hadn't spoken in years, I figured I was the only friend he had left. I was worried for his well-being, and that's why I decided to go.

"When Wallace and I arrived, Greg was in severe distress. He was sweating, pacing around non-stop, and talking to someone who wasn't there. When I tried to call 911, he took the phone from me, threw it across the living room, ripped the cord out of the wall, then ran out the patio door.

"Wallace and I ran after him, and we spent the next hour trying to convince him to come back into the house. He was disoriented, and he kept saying he had a knife. We didn't know for sure, but we were afraid he might hurt us or himself if we approached him. That went on until you and Candace arrived."

Robin and I stare at Daniel in disbelief. Then she turns to me. "So, when you woke up, Gen, Wallace was gone? He left without telling you where he went?"

"Exactly. I found Candace sleeping on our couch. I don't know what she was thinking. If Greg was frantic like Dan says he was, how could she think it was a good idea for her to leave Wallace alone with him? She's so careless! I'm just as angry with Wallace for thinking it was a good idea to go there without telling me and for leaving Alaina under Candace's supervision! I know I was in the house, but he was the one who was supposed to be taking care of her. Candace could've done something to Alaina while I was asleep!" My stomach turns at the thought of Alaina or Wallace getting harmed.

"This night could've been a lot worse," Robin says. "You all could've died."

Dan lowers his head. "I know. I realize that."

After getting some coffee, we return to the waiting room. Only Norman is there. Everyone else is gone.

"The doctor came in while you were away," he says. "They told us that Greg didn't make it. Rhea arrived a few minutes ago, and they're all in his room right now, saying their final goodbyes."

The three of us take a seat next to Norman, waiting for the others to return. Hundreds of thoughts are racing through my mind. I'm not surprised that Greg is dead. In fact, it's shocking that he survived this long. I thought for sure they were going to declare him dead at the scene. I suppose that the "disease," as he put it, wanted to keep him prisoner even longer. As horrible as it may seem, I'm relieved he's gone. I can't imagine the suffering he would have gone through if he had survived. He could've had brain damage or been paralyzed. This fate is so much kinder to him than either of those scenarios.

My thoughts are interrupted by Alaina crying. I try to soothe her, then check her diaper to see if she needs to be changed.

"I'll be right back," I say, standing up.

"Do you need any help?" Robin asks.

"No, I'll be fine. I just need a minute, if that's okay."

"Of course," Robin replies.

I walk down the hallway to the bathroom. On the way, I notice the Browne family in one of the hospital rooms. The door is shut, but a large window allows me to see inside. Wallace is at the foot of the bed. He looks like he's crying and pleading over his brother's lifeless body. My heart shatters for him. Candace and Rhea are in the corner. They look emotionless. I wish I could say I'm surprised, but I'm not. Neither Rhea nor Candace have shed a tear since the day I met them. It's eerie to watch their expressionless faces while Wallace has a complete breakdown over his brother's death. I want to barge in and yell at Candace and Rhea and comfort Wallace, but I restrain myself. They need this time together as a family regardless of how much I disapprove of their lack of sympathy.

Once in the bathroom, I change and feed Alaina. I've been breastfeeding and pumping exclusively, and it's going well. I pump a few times between 7:00 p.m. and midnight, which provides enough milk to last most of the night when Wallace feeds her. I'm an over supplier, so sometimes I need to pump in the middle of the night just to relieve the engorgement.

Alaina falls asleep while she's feeding. Before moving her, I examine her little features. She looks so much like Wallace, it's uncanny. Watching her sleep so peacefully makes me smile. She's completely unaware of the chaos we've all experienced this evening.

I can't help but worry about her, though. When Wallace was diagnosed, I asked the psychiatrist about the chances of our children inheriting a mental illness from their father's side of the family. He said it was highly unlikely, and that Wallace's family's history was mostly caused by shared or generational trauma. Since my side of the family has no history of mental illness, as long as we prevent our children from experiencing significant trauma during childhood, the risk remains low.

Wallace and I debated having children for some time because of this fear. Once we saw how well he responded to the medication, though, we decided to take the risk. I'm happy we did because now we have our beautiful daughter, but I'm still scared that she might be affected, especially after the events that unfolded tonight. Sure, we can shield her now, but it might not be as easy once she's older. Regardless, I'll do everything in my power to ensure that she isn't exposed to the trauma that her father had to endure. I'm going to protect her no matter what.

On my way back to the waiting area, I cross paths with Wallace and his family as they leave Greg's hospital room. Rhea and Candace just walk past me toward the exit, but Wallace runs to me and gives me a hug.

When he pulls back, I look into his eyes. His expression is unreadable, apart from the tear stains on his cheeks. "I'm so sorry," I say, giving him an apologetic look. "I'm so sorry for everything that's happened. I just hope you know this isn't your fault."

"Thanks, Gem. I'm just glad that you and Laina are safe." He takes Alaina from me and holds her against his chest, kissing her on her forehead. "I'm so sorry, baby. For everything I've done tonight. I promise I'll never leave you like that again." He's speaking to the baby, but I know he's talking to me too. I put a hand on his shoulder.

"What happened with Rhea and Candace?" I ask. "They seemed upset with you."

His face hardens. "I told them that I never want to see them again."

Chapter 28

"Can you please tell me exactly what happened tonight?" I ask Wallace.

We're on our way back home from the hospital. I decided to drive since I'm not sure of Wallace's mental state after everything he's gone through tonight. Alaina is still asleep in her carrier.

"I know it was stupid of me to go without telling you, but I was worried that you would discourage me from going, and I didn't want to do something against your judgment. It was easier for me this way."

"But how could you leave Alaina under Candace's supervision? You know she can't be trusted."

"I know. I'm sorry. I figured she would never try anything with you in the house. I wasn't thinking straight. I don't know where my head was at." Wallace looks down. "I just needed answers."

I raise an eyebrow. "Answers to what?"

"I needed to know if it was true. If Greg's mental illness destroyed him. I definitely got my answer." He looks out the window. "Candace called me tonight and said he was doing well. She said he might've had a chance to get better. She lied to me, clearly. I don't know what her goal was. She was probably hoping that Greg would succeed at throwing me off the bridge with him."

"It's not the first time that Candace has done something like this to you," I reply. "I'm not surprised she would say something like that. However, I'm surprised she told me where you were. She was so quick to run after you guys when she realized where you might be. If she wanted you both dead, she wouldn't have helped me find you. If it wasn't for her, Greg could've dragged you off the bridge with him.

"After tonight, I realize who Candace is," he says. "She's exactly like my mother. She can't feel empathy or any other emotion. She tries to act as if she has a conscience, and I know she wants to be capable of caring, but she isn't. What you saw tonight is a perfect example of her trying to act like she cared about my well-being. But I know she wants me dead. Otherwise, she wouldn't have set me up like that—again. Her and Mom are simply apathetic. Neither of them showed an ounce of emotion while Greg's lifeless body laid beneath them. They're monsters, and I no longer want them in our lives."

I can feel the hurt in his voice, and I agree with everything he says. Despite their actions, I can't even imagine how difficult it must be for him to let go of the only family he has left.

"I'm so sorry baby. I'm so incredibly sorry."

"It's okay. You and Alaina are all I need. I'm better off without them."

I hope he's right.

Chapter 29

A few months have gone by since the night Greg died. Dan, Wallace, Candace, and I were all obligated to provide a statement to the police regarding the circumstances that led to Greg's death. After each of our statements checked out, they were able to rule the death as accidental, even though I would consider it a suicide.

I was worried that Candace was going to accuse Daniel of pushing Greg on purpose, but if she did, the police didn't buy it. We haven't seen or heard from Candace or Rhea since that night. I thought that Wallace would be devastated after everything that happened, but he's been doing quite well this past month. He took it hard at first, but I think he feels relieved from no longer having Rhea or Candace in his life.

Neither of them showed up at Greg's funeral. Wallace had to plan everything, since Greg didn't really have anyone else in his life to do it. It was a sad funeral; Wallace and my family were the only ones there. It upsets me that Greg never got the help or support that he deserved. I believe that Rhea and Candace failed him. If there would have been an earlier intervention, especially from Rhea, maybe he would have been alive and doing well for himself today. Instead, when he was admitted, they disregarded his existence. They preferred to pretend that he was a successful business owner in Winnipeg rather than try to help him work toward recovery. They let him rot in there, all alone, all the while lying to Wallace and everyone else about what happened to him. It's not fair that Greg had to suffer like that for so many years. I wonder how he was able to convince the doctors at the hospital that he was well enough to be released. I can't imagine the act he had to put on for years before they agreed to let him go. It must've taken everything out of him to play that persona for so long. No wonder he reached a breaking point so soon after getting out. That poor man was damaged beyond repair. I hope he has found peace after living such an unfair life. Wallace mourned his brother's death, but I think his grief stemmed mostly from him losing the only chance he had to have someone in his life who understood him and what he went through.

On our way home that night, when Wallace revealed that Candace had convinced him that Greg was doing well, Wallace probably held on to the hope of having his brother back in his life. The disappointed look on his face after he told me that he found Greg acting irrationally broke me. All of his hope vanished. I pray every day that our family is enough to make him happy. I don't want him to feel alone in this world. I'm determined to show him how loved he is and how we can break this daunting cycle of trauma.

...

I hear Wallace walk down the hallway while I'm sitting on the sofa in our living room. He's holding Alaina in one of his arms. "Look who's up from her nap!" he says, grinning. Alaina smiles when she sees me.

"Come here my beautiful girl," I say. "Did you have a good nap?"

Wallace places her into my arms, and I put her on my lap. Alaina just turned five months old. She's sleeping through the night, and she just started on solid food a few days ago. She's a good baby, but it took her time to get there. She had colic for about six weeks, which made her scream almost every night. After that, we found out that she has an allergy to cow's milk, but it took three weeks of fussing and rashes before we realized it. I tried giving up dairy entirely to continue breastfeeding, but eventually, I gave up because her symptoms weren't going away. Apparently, there's dairy in almost everything. So, we started giving her a special formula. It was a nightmare to go through all that, so it feels like such a blessing that she's such a happy baby the majority of the time.

"Are you almost ready to go?" I ask Wallace.

"Yes. I just need to brush my teeth, and we can head out."

We're meeting Michael and Victoria for lunch. My mother offered to watch Alaina for us in the meantime. We've only been away from Alaina once since Greg died.

I became paranoid after that night, and I was too afraid to let anyone else watch her. It's an irrational fear because I trust my family members completely, but I've still been hesitant. I've forgiven Wallace for allowing Candace to watch her, but ever since then, I wake up at every sound I hear at night. I'm terrified that something might happen to her if she isn't in my care at all times.

I realize how unhealthy that is. Eventually, I'll have to return to work, and Wallace will have to watch her during the day while I'm gone. I'm doing everything I can to ease this anxiety, which is why I'm allowing my mother to watch her while we go to lunch.

Victoria and Michael know everything about our past. Greg's death showed up on the news, and they had a lot of questions. I love them both to death, but they can be nosey, and they don't recognize when they ask questions that are too personal or inappropriate. I figured they would find out eventually, and the closer I got to them, the more I felt that they deserved to know the truth about everything anyway. So, one night, I invited them over while Wallace was at work, and I told them everything, from the moment I met Wallace to the day Greg died. To say they were shocked is an understatement. They were baffled. It felt good not to have to keep any secrets from them. I know they won't spread any gossip about our family at school.

When we arrive at the restaurant, Mike and Vic are already seated at a table. They stand up and wave for us to join them, giving Wallace and I a hug before we all sit down.

"It's been too long!" Michael says. "We've missed you guys!"

"I know. We've missed you too," Wallace says. "We've been so busy with Alaina, we've forgotten to prioritize our adult time lately."

"Well, it looks like we're going to be in the same boat as you soon!" Vic says with excitement.

My eyes widen. "What do you mean Vic?" I ask with a big smile on my face.

"We've just finalized the adoption! We bring our baby home next week!"

"Oh my God! Congratulations!" I exclaim. I get up to hug them both.

"This is so exciting!" Wallace says. "I'm so happy for you both."

Michael and Victoria have been going through the adoption process for months. Through their adoption agency, they found a five-year-old boy named Tanner, who is in foster care. They've been preparing their home to welcome him. It took them a long time to get approved.

"We're nervous to have him under our care, but we're so ready," Vic says. "We've been waiting for years to become parents. This little boy is our miracle baby." Mike and Vic hold each other's hands. Michael kisses her on the lips while slightly tearing up.

"I'm so grateful that I get to share this happiness with you, my love," he says.

She gazes at him with admiration. "I wouldn't want to do this with anyone else, babe." She kisses him again.

Wallace and I smile at each other. Their lives are so different from ours, but I see such a resemblance in the love that they share for each other. Their bond seems unbreakable, just like ours.

"You're both going to make amazing parents," I say. "I can't wait to meet him. Can we throw you an adoption baby shower?"

"Absolutely!" Vic replies.

After a nice lunch, we hug Victoria and Michael and then head back to the car.

When we arrive at my parents' house, Alaina's little face lights up. My mom has her doing tummy time on a little play mat she has from when we were babies. It looks to be about forty years old. Knowing my mom, she's disinfected it about a thousand times, so I'm not worried.

"She was an absolute dream! Alaina is the sweetest baby I've ever met. She needs to come visit Grandma and Grandpa more often. Right, Bob?" She turns to my dad, who is sitting in his easy chair at the end of the living room.

"Absolutely!" he replies, standing. "She's the most precious baby. She giggled and smiled the entire time. It makes me want to have another." He pokes my mom's side and winks.

"You'll have to find a lady much younger than me if you want another baby!" she says. "My ovaries have turned into dust at this point."

My father laughs. "No, but seriously, Alaina is an absolute joy. You've done well with her so far," he says.

"Thank you so much, Mr. Daley, but it's all Alaina," Wallace replies. "She's naturally perfect. We just got lucky." He smiles at me.

Once we're in the car, ready to head home, Wallace turns toward me. "Gem?"

"Yes?"

"I don't know if it's just the high I feel for Vic and Mike's exciting news or if it's the conversation we just had with your parents, but—"

"You want to have another baby?"

"Yes!"

I nod in excitement, and Wallace leans over and kisses me while Alaina giggles in the back seat.

Chapter 30

1999

It took almost another year before I decided to get pregnant again. I didn't get a positive test until July 1997. Alaina is almost three years old now, and we also have an eight-month old son, Lance. We named him after Wallace, but we've agreed to call him Lance as a nickname. It's the only way I accepted to name him after his father. I have nothing against the name, but I've always disliked it when parents name their children after themselves. I feel like it takes away from the child's identity, but it meant a lot to Wallace, so we compromised.

I gave birth to Lance last April. Robin got pregnant at around the same time, and she gave birth to her daughter, Nora, last August. Raising our children together has been the best thing ever. I've always wanted my children to grow up with cousins who are close in age. Since Dan and Linda had their children a lot earlier than we did, we never had the chance to raise our kids together. From the moment Lance and Nora were born, Robin's and my relationship has grown stronger than ever. I helped her and Norman a lot during the newborn stage since I already had the experience, and she really appreciated any advice I gave. It's so nice having my sister also be my best friend.

Since my maternity leave is only six months, I've been back at work for almost two months, but now I'm on Christmas break for the next two weeks. Wallace stays with the kids during the day while I work, and I take over when I get home.

It's been almost three years since Mike and Vic adopted Tanner. In that time, they also adopted his older sister, Sienna. Since becoming parents, they have been the happiest we've ever seen them. Their children love spending time with Alaina and Lance, so they come over frequently.

Soon after Lance was born, I've noticed a slight change in Wallace's mood. He seems to get slightly impatient with Lance, which is something that I've never seen him do with Alaina, especially when she was a baby. At first, I thought it may have been because he wanted to be tougher on his boy, but I noticed the same behaviour soon after with Alaina as well.

One night a few weeks ago, he was picking up a late shift at work. Right before he left at 10:00 p.m., he woke Alaina and accused her of stealing his car keys. He yelled so aggressively that she started crying. I had to scream at him to get him to stop.

Alaina has developed a habit recently where she picks up toys and other objects and "stores them away" in random spots. We both thought it was adorable at first, but not after Wallace convinced himself that she had hidden his keys from him. Right after upsetting her, he found them in a drawer that she couldn't even reach. She never touched his keys; he had simply misplaced them. Seeing such behaviour from Wallace felt odd. Everything in our lives is going fine right now, so I don't understand why he would have such outbursts.

This evening, I stay up after the kids are put to bed. I read a book while I'm waiting for Wallace to get home from work, so we can watch a movie. He's supposed to come home around 10:00.

My salary has gone up significantly in the last few years, so Wallace has been able to reduce his schedule to thirty hours a week. After Lance was born, Wallace found it difficult to work eight-hour shifts after taking care of the two kids all day. With our calculations, we will be able to make it work and still save up a good amount of money each month.

After nine long years, I was finally able to pay off my student loans. Wallace still has about two thousand dollars of his schooling debt to pay, but one less payment per month has helped us significantly. After three years of saving, we finally have enough for a down payment on a house. We're set to move into our new home in January. We've been staying in the same apartment since we got married, and we have wanted to buy a house before Lance gets out of his crib. He's sleeping in our room right now, and the apartment is too small for a family of four. Although winter isn't the best time of year for house hunting, we found a beautiful house at a reasonable price that we couldn't pass up. It's an average-size, three-bedroom bungalow, and it has a huge backyard. It's perfect for our little family. I'm so proud of this milestone that we're just weeks away from reaching.

"Hi Gem," Wallace says as he walks through the front door.

"Hi, babe! How was work?"

"It was fine," he says, his voice sounding flat.

"Are you in the mood to watch a movie?" I ask, raising my eyebrows hopefully.

"Not really, baby. I'm tired. I think I should just go to bed," he says, barely looking in my direction. He heads straight toward the fridge and takes out a beer. "Well, after this beer," he adds.

"Is everything okay? Did something happen at work?"

"No! I already told you it was fine!"

I lean farther back into the sofa, startled by his reaction. He looks at me, and his expression softens. "I'm so sorry, my Gem. It's just been a long day. This time of year isn't easy for me. I shouldn't have taken it out on you."

He sits down next to me and pulls me into him, resting his chin on top of my head. "I'm sorry for snapping at you. I love you so much. I'm sorry." He speaks rapidly, and his breathing quickens. His reaction worries me, but I try not to think too much about it.

"It's okay, I understand. I'm sorry if I pushed you too far." I regret the words as soon as they escape my mouth. I didn't push him too far. He's the one who has such a short fuse lately. I understand that this time of year is hard for him, but that doesn't excuse his shitty behaviour. Despite my opinions, I can't get myself to speak my mind. I just want to have a peaceful evening.

"We can watch a movie if you want to," he whispers.

"No, honey, it's okay," I reply while rubbing his arm. "Let's just go to bed."

After he finishes his beer, we make our way to the bedroom.

...

The next morning, I wake up at around 7:00 a.m. to the sound of Lance baby-talking. Wallace is asleep next to me.

"Good morning, my handsome boy!" I say to Lance. He reaches his arms out for me to pick him up. I take him from his crib and go to the living room. I've already started packing things up for when we move in a few weeks, but we still have a few coffee mugs in the cupboards. I only started drinking coffee after having kids. The exhaustion is something I never really get over. I just learn to function even when I feel like a zombie.

I place Lance in his high chair, then turn on the coffee pot. I make oatmeal for Lance and mix in some of my breast milk. Thankfully, Lance doesn't share the same allergy that his sister had when she was a baby. I'm cutting up some strawberries and placing them in a bowl when I hear tiny footsteps from across the hall.

"Good morning my sweet Alaina."

"Good morning, Mama." Alaina pulls out a chair and struggles to climb onto it. When she succeeds, she places her arms on the table, waiting to be served. I give her a bowl of strawberries, then I give Lance his oatmeal, topped with strawberries. I also put some bread in the toaster. Alaina loves toast with raspberry jam in the morning.

After breakfast and a short playtime, I put Lance and Alaina down for their naps at around 9:00. It takes them less than ten minutes to fall asleep. They're good sleepers. Wallace is still in bed, so I go take a shower. As I'm brushing my teeth afterward, I notice the toothpaste tube is almost empty. I look into our linen closet, but I can't find a replacement. Wallace put away the groceries last week, and he has a tendency to place everything in different spots from where they usually go. I open the medicine cabinet, and I'm stunned to find different bottles, filled with pills. I take one from the cabinet and hold it closer to my face, so I can read the label. Lithium. Wallace gets a refill every month for his medication. He went to the pharmacy just a week ago when he told me that he was going to run out of pills. How come there are three full bottles of his medication?

It can't be, I think. All of his recent outbursts suddenly make sense.

"Gem? Are you in there?" Wallace calls out from outside the bathroom door. "I need to pee. Can I come in?" I try to control my anger before deciding what to do next. When Wallace opens the door and notices the bottle in my hand, he freezes.

"Gem. You have to let me explain," he says. I throw the bottle at his chest in anger and I walk straight past him, ignoring him. I head into the bedroom and start to pack a bag for me and the kids.

"Gem, what are you doing? Please don't leave!" He grabs my arm, but I yank it out of his grasp.

"God damn it, Wallace, for the sake of our marriage, let me leave. I need time to think. I'm bringing the kids because I don't trust you right now."

He steps back and looks down. "Please give me the chance to explain. You don't understand."

"Maybe I don't! But you made me a promise. You vowed that you would never do this! How could you put your family at risk like this? After all this time! I did everything I could to prevent this! Everything! How can you fail me like this?"

I can't allow myself to stay and hear him out. I need to leave before I say something that I'm going to regret. "I'm going to stay at my parents' place until I calm down. I'm taking the kids with me. I'll be back before Christmas Eve. I'm sorry, but I can't do this right now." I can't bring myself to look him in the eyes because I know the look he has on his face will make me feel guilty, and I can't allow that right now.

"Okay," he replies.

I think back at the time that he almost killed himself, and panic runs through me. "Are you going to be okay?" I ask, still avoiding eye contact. He knows exactly what I mean without me having to say it.

"Yes, Gem. I'll be fine. Just please come back. I'm really sorry."

Once I get to my parents' house, I call Wallace's friend, Justin, and I beg him to spend the night at our place to make sure Wallace doesn't try to hurt himself. Justin reassures me that he'll be there and to not worry. He says he'll call me if anything happens.

My mom makes me a cup of tea while I set the kids down. I placed Lance, who is still asleep, onto the sofa, and I put Alaina on the floor in the living room. I give her Fluffy, which I had stuffed in my purse. She occupies herself while I sit next to Lance.

My mom hands me a cup of tea and sits down on the chair in front of me. "Dad is out for an early lunch with his old mining buddies. He should be home around two," she says. "Now, sweetheart, tell me what's going on."

I spend the next thirty minutes or so explaining everything to her—the odd behaviour that I've been observing, the outbursts, and the pills I found in the medicine cabinet.

"Oh, baby. How could he do that? Wallace usually has such a sound mind despite the mental illness he struggled with all of those years ago." My mom knows a lot of things about Wallace, but she's not completely aware of the circumstances that surrounded Greg's death. She thinks it was an accident, and she doesn't know anything beyond that. I keep that in mind as I listen to her advice. "You know Wallace is a good man," she says. "Otherwise, you wouldn't have married him!"

"I know, Mom. I know he's a good man. But I made him promise me before we got married that he would never stop taking his medication. He just broke the promise that's at the foundation of our marriage! How can I get past this?"

"By loving him through it, sweetheart. When you started dating him, you had so many concerns about his mental health, but you chose to love him regardless. You can't give up on him now. You knew the risks before you agreed to marry him. Now he needs your support more than ever." Even though she doesn't know the whole story, my mother has a point. How can I turn my back on him after nine years of marriage and two children? I have more than just myself to think about now.

"Maybe I should hear him out before jumping to conclusions," I say after taking a deep breath.

"I think that's the best idea," she replies, placing her hand on my shoulder.

...

The next morning, I wake up around 6:30 and pick up Lance from the playpen that my mom has set up in this room. My parents' house has two spare bedrooms, but Alaina wanted to sleep in my bed last night, and I wanted Lance to stay in the same room as me. Alaina is still asleep, so I sneak out of bed and go to the living room, so I can breastfeed Lance. I'm planning to head home as soon as possible, so I won't have time to make him breakfast before I leave.

When I walk into the living room, my mom is seated on the sofa. "Good morning, Mom. Couldn't sleep?" I ask while taking a seat beside her.

"Good morning, honey. No. I can't sleep whenever I have a child who's in distress. I stay up all night worrying. Your father's snoring doesn't help the situation." She laughs. I manage to smile.

"I'm sorry for putting you through this, Mama. I panicked and didn't know where else to go."

"Don't ever apologize to me, baby, I'll worry about you until my last breath. That's my job." She smiles. "You'll know when your babies get older. You'll sacrifice anything for them, but that sacrifice will be sleep about ninety-eight percent of the time."

"I feel like I already have an idea. From the moment Alaina was born, I've had this instinct to protect her from anything, no matter what. That instinct grew even stronger after giving birth to Lance. These babies are my life." I grow emotional as I look at Lance. "Why do I always have this feeling that something bad will happen to them?" My voice breaks.

"Baby, that's what it is to be a mother. All of your fears, your worries, are now directly linked to your children. They're a part of you, and you'll always feel the need to save them before they even need saving." She leans her head on my shoulder.

"Thank you, Mom. For everything you've sacrificed. I love you so much."

"I love you too, sweetheart. Always."

After an hour, we're finally ready to return home. On the way there, I contemplate what I'm going to say to Wallace.

When we arrive at the apartment, Wallace is at the front door, waiting for us. He takes Lance out of my arms and grabs the diaper bag. I take Alaina's hand as we walk inside.

"Honey, go play in your room for a bit," I say to her, "but keep the door open, so I can see you, please." She heads straight to her room.

I sit on a chair in the living room. Wallace places Lance in the bouncer, then sits on the sofa across from me.

"What time did Justin leave?" I ask.

"Five this morning. He had to work. Thank you for coming back."

"Why did you break your promise?" I ask.

"I know how it seems, Gem. I know it scares you. But I promise, I don't need them anymore."

I raise an eyebrow. "How can you not need them anymore? Your mental illness can't just disappear, Wallace."

"I know, but I want to try a different approach from medication. I've been off the meds for three months now, and there have been no signs of things getting bad again." There's a hopeful look in his eyes, but I'm far from convinced.

"How can you say that? You've been irritable lately. You lashed out on Alaina for something she didn't even do, and you lack patience toward her and Lance."

"I know, and I'm sorry. Irritability is a side effect of weaning off the medication. I promise it will get better."

"I'm not sure your promises mean much to me anymore," I say, crossing my arms.

"You don't understand, Gem! Those pills, they numb me! I can't do it anymore. I haven't felt like myself in years. When you gave birth to Alaina and Lance, I felt as if my joy was numbed. I don't want to miss out on those feelings. I don't want to be like my mother and Candace."

I'm shocked by his revelation. "You appeared overjoyed both times I gave birth. Was that all an act?"

"No, no. Of course I was happy. You don't understand! It's just that it feels as if my emotions are far away. Almost too far from my reach. They're there, but I don't feel the full effects. I've been living that way for years, so I've been able to mimic what I should be feeling. It's the medication that's doing this to me. I've been doing research, and it's possible for me to use therapy as a treatment instead to ensure my mood remains stabilized."

He gets up from the sofa and crouches in front of me, taking my hands in his. I understand where he is coming from. Ever since we got married, I've noticed that his medication appears to have slightly changed his behaviour. He's a lot calmer, less passionate, and less sentimental. I would be lying if I didn't say I missed those parts of him, but I figured it was a small price to pay to ensure his stability.

"Please, my Gem. Please let me at least try. If I start to feel bad again, I promise I'll go back on the medication. If I don't, you can leave with the kids. I won't fight it."

I'm hesitant to agree, but I don't really have a choice. I don't want to leave him, and I believe he deserves the chance to find an alternative to medication. I just hope he keeps his word.

"Okay. You can give it a try. I want to support you, I do. But you shouldn't have kept it from me. If you would've come to me about this, I wouldn't have gotten so upset."

"I know, my Gem. I'm sorry. I didn't want to disappoint you. I wanted to prove to you that I could do it before telling you. I'm sorry." He kisses my cheek. I pull him into a hug and run my fingers through his hair.

"It's okay, babe. We can give it a chance," I say.

I hope I'm not making a big mistake.

PART TWO

Chapter 31

2004

Something is severely wrong with Wallace.

Our fourteenth wedding anniversary was just yesterday, but Wallace was too sick to celebrate. He's had flu-like symptoms all week, and he's gotten even worse since yesterday. When he woke up this morning, he had an empty look in his eyes, and he could barely speak without slurring his words. The only way he got out of bed was by listening to my step-by-step instructions on what to do. I had to tell him to lift himself up off the bed and to walk into the bathroom. Once he made it to the bathroom, he just stood there, motionless, until I told him to get undressed, get into the shower, and turn on the water. I left him there while I went to check on the kids.

Our lives have changed in the last five years. When Wallace stopped taking his medication, he was serious about going to therapy to treat his mental illness. The therapy seems to have worked because he hasn't had an episode of mania or depression since. He continues his sessions regularly, even though he believes he no longer needs them. I've been encouraging him to continue as a precaution.

I got pregnant again about five months after we moved into our new home. After Wallace stopped his medication, I didn't want to have any more children. I've always wanted three, but I was worried that something bad was going to happen, and I didn't want to risk having another baby. When I accidentally got pregnant just a few months later, I was terrified. But I've been grateful ever since we welcomed another beautiful daughter, Maya, into our family in April of 2001. She's a true blessing, and she's proof that everything happens for a reason. However, I did make Wallace get a vasectomy as soon as she was born. Our family is complete with Maya, and we can't afford to have another baby.

Wallace is still in the shower, and it's been over fifteen minutes. I go into the bathroom and draw the curtain to check on him. He's facing the wall of the shower, and the water isn't even touching his body. He has goosebumps all over. "Wallace! You need to step under the shower head!" I tell him, concerned. Without looking at me, he steps to his right, and the water trickles down his body. Instead of continuing to tell him what to do, I wash his hair and his body for him, getting soaked in the process. Then I tell him to step out of the shower, and I towel him off.

I walk him back to the bedroom and help him put on his boxers. After I sit him on the bed, I go downstairs to call Robin.

When she answers, I hear a screaming baby in the background. Robin had a second daughter two years after mine, and she just turned a year old.

"Sorry. Chloe is yelling too much. Let me leave the room, so I can hear you better." I hear her tumble around until a door shuts, then there's complete silence.

"There we go, much better. What's up, sis?"

"Something's wrong with Wallace. He woke up this morning acting super strange. He's been sick all week, but now he's even worse than yesterday. I think I need to bring him to the hospital. Can you come over and check him out? I want a second opinion." I can't keep the panic out of my voice.

"Of course. Let me get Norman and the kids ready. We can watch Alaina, Lance, and Maya for you at your house while you take him to the hospital."

"Thank you so much. Love you. See you soon."

"Love you too. Bye."

When I hang up, I turn around and see Alaina standing behind me.

"What's wrong with Daddy?" she asks, looking nervous.

"I don't know, sweetie. I think your Daddy is really sick. I'm going to bring him to the hospital today to see how the doctors can help him."

"Why is he just sitting there, not moving and staring at nothing?" Lance asks as he comes up behind her.

"I don't know, sweetheart. Alaina, can you take Lance back up to your and Maya's room to play? Auntie Robin and Uncle Norm are going to come over in a few minutes. You can come out when they arrive."

Alaina takes Lance by the hand and walks him up the stairs toward her bedroom. She distracts him from asking any more questions about Wallace. Alaina is only eight, but she acts like a grown-up sometimes. She worries a lot, which makes her responsible too. She's taken on the role of a big sister well.

I follow them upstairs to check on Wallace. He's sitting in the same position that I left him in.

"Wallace, please get up," I say. He does what I ask, but he's still staring into space. I help him walk down the stairs, then I sit him on the couch. Minutes later, Robin and Norman arrive with their daughters.

"Auntie Genny!" Nora runs up to me and hugs me. Then she runs up the stairs to join her cousins. Chloe wobbles closely behind her. I pick her up before she gets to the steps and give her a kiss on the cheek.

"Hi, Wallace." Norman waves in Wallace's direction. I can tell by Robin and Norman's expressions that they are shocked by Wallace's state.

"Oh my God, Gen. What the hell is going on with him?" Robin whispers in my ear.

"That's what I need to find out."

"Maybe you should bring him to the clinic first before going to the hospital and waiting for hours in the emergency room," Norman suggests.

"You're probably right. I'll go there first to see if they can tell me what's going on."

"Good idea," Robin and Norman both say at once.

I give Chloe back to Robin, then I run upstairs to pack a bag in case we end up at the hospital. I hug and kiss the kids, then head back down. I tell Wallace to get up from the couch, and Norman helps him put his shoes on. Then we leave the house and head for the clinic.

There's no waiting time at the clinic. We got into an examination room right away.

"What seems to be the problem, Mr. Browne?" the doctor asks Wallace. Wallace is still staring into the distance, and he appears completely unaware of his surroundings. "Mr. Browne?" the doctor says. He puts his chart down and puts on a pair of gloves. He feels around Wallace's neck, checks his lungs and heart, and flashes a light into his eyes.

"You have a history of mental illness. Is that correct Mr. Browne?" The doctor steps back from Wallace and leans on the counter beside the examination table. He takes a pen out of his white lab coat's pocket and starts writing on his notepad.

"Yes, but that isn't what's happening. Something else is wrong!" I snap. The doctor ignores me.

"It says here that you stopped taking your medication to treat your manic depression. Sorry, I mean, bipolar disorder." In recent years, the medical terminology for Wallace's psychiatric disorder has changed from manic depression to bipolar disorder to reduce stigma. People tend to link the word "manic" or "mania" to "maniac," which basically means *crazy*.

"Yes, he stopped using his medication over five years ago. He's been going to therapy instead, and he hasn't had a mania or depression episode in years! You need to believe me when I say this isn't what's going on with him!" I'm growing agitated. When Wallace had his first depression episode after we started dating, he told me that he didn't want to get any help because he was worried that having a label would cause him to be treated unfairly. After all these years, I finally understand what he meant.

The doctor continues to write on his notepad, not looking up at me while I talk to him.

"Mr. Browne, are you depressed?" the doctor asks, looking at him. Wallace doesn't answer. The doctor finally looks in my direction.

"How long was he on lithium?" he asks.

"Nine years."

"I see. You know, after being on a mood-stabilizing medication like lithium for all those years, it takes a long time for its effects to leave your system. It's possible that he is, just now, starting a depression after all these years. I suggest you make an appointment with his psychiatrist. Otherwise, I see a perfectly healthy adult man in front of me." He stands up straight and reaches his arm out for a handshake. I refuse to take his hand.

"This isn't depression. I've seen him depressed before, multiple times, and not once did he act like this! You have to believe there's something wrong with him!"

"Depression can take lots of different forms, ma'am. You need to calm down and call his psychiatrist to make an appointment."

I've heard enough. "Wallace, get up!" I shout. I help him get off the table and then walk him out of the room. I'm so furious, I feel like I could carry him all the way to the car by myself.

Once we're in the car, I call Robin. "The doctor doesn't believe anything is wrong. He thinks Wallace is depressed. I'm taking him to the hospital. Are you okay to stay with the kids until I get back?"

"Of course, Gen. Don't worry about us. Just go make sure he's taken care of. Keep us posted."

On the way to the hospital, Wallace becomes increasingly unresponsive. When I ask him to do something, he can no longer do it. He's still staring into emptiness, slouched over, his seatbelt is the only thing that's preventing him from falling forward and hitting his face on the dash.

When we arrive at the emergency room, two male nurses have to help get him out of the car because I can't move him. I follow them into the emergency department as they push Wallace in a wheelchair.

A few minutes later, a doctor starts examining him. "Hi, Mr. and Mrs. Browne, I'm Dr. Embrun." Wallace is lying on the bed, staring at the ceiling. As soon as the doctor examines his eyes with his small flashlight, he looks over at the nurses. "Signs of encephalitis and cerebral edema. We need to take him to the ICU immediately," he says.

Within seconds, they're rolling the bed out of the room. "What's going on?" I ask, panicking.

"There's inflammation and swelling on your husband's brain. It's pushing against his skull, causing pressure. If we don't relieve that pressure soon, it could be dangerous or even fatal."

Chapter 32

My heart is practically pounding out of my chest. I can't believe this is happening to him. Dr. Embrun follows Wallace and the nurses into the ICU. He tells me to sit in the waiting room and that he'll come back with an update as soon as possible.

When I call Robin to tell her what's happening, she sounds horrified. I can barely get the words out as I struggle to breathe.

"Do you need me to come see you?" Robin asks.

"No, it's okay. I'll call Dad instead. I need to tell him what's going on."

"Okay, just let me know."

"Thanks." I hang up and dial my father's number.

When he picks up, I tell him what's going on, and he agrees to meet me at the hospital.

All I can think about is how badly I need my mom right now. She passed away when Maya was just a few weeks old. She was diagnosed with an untreatable cancer a few years before she passed, soon after Lance was born. Losing her was one of the most difficult things I've ever been through. It took my dad a long time to move forward after her death. For the first two years, he was drowning in grief. Only after Chloe was born did we finally start seeing some life in him again. I'm grateful that my dad is still around to help me navigate through this. After seeing him grieve my mother, I don't know how I would survive if Wallace didn't make it. I'm hoping more than anything that he pulls through.

My dad arrives at the hospital twenty minutes later, and stays by my side while I cry hysterically, terrified of what's going to happen to Wallace. He rubs my back, not saying a word. His presence is comforting during a time like this.

We wait at the hospital for hours. Wallace was admitted at around 11:00 a.m., and it's now 9:00 p.m., but Dr. Embrun still hasn't come by with an update. A few nurses have told us that he's still working on stabilizing Wallace.

My father goes to my house, so he can take over from Robin and watch the kids. Norman goes home with their children since he works tomorrow, and Robin comes to the hospital to wait with me. She called in sick to work for the next few days, so she can stay with me for as long as I need.

Two hours later, Dr. Embrun finally comes out to talk to us. "Your husband is still in critical condition. We were unable to reduce the swelling, and we're concerned that he might suffer significant damage to his brain. When we took an MRI, we were able to confirm that he has encephalitis, a condition caused by a virus. We administered an antiviral drug to treat him, but he had an adverse reaction to the medication. He started getting hives all over his body, so we had to stop the treatment immediately." He pauses, looking defeated. "I'm sorry to say, Mrs. Browne, but without the antiviral medication, we might not be able to get the swelling to go down in time to save him. There's a chance he might not wake up."

Hearing those words makes my knees go weak. Robin holds onto me and sits me back in the chair, preventing me from falling to the floor. I'm crying hysterically. This can't be happening. I can't lose my husband.

A faint memory comes to mind. I remember him having a similar allergic reaction at the hospital the night he attempted to end his life. They had done an MRI to make sure his brain wasn't affected by the lack of oxygen he sustained from the hemorrhaging.

I wipe my tears with my sleeve and clear my throat before speaking.

"Wait, did you inject dye in his IV when you took him to get an MRI?" I ask.

"Yes, we did," Dr. Embrun confirms.

"He's allergic to the dye. It causes him to break out in hives. You have to try the antiviral medication again!"

"Thank you, Mrs. Browne. We'll do that right away," Dr. Embrun says as he runs back to the ICU.

"Thank God you remembered that, Gen," Robin says.

"I know," I reply, my heart racing.

I place my face into my hand, and let out a deep sigh. Then I close my eyes and pray for Wallace's recovery. If there's anything the universe, God, or whatever else can do for me, it's to make sure my husband makes it out of this alive.

Chapter 33

After a long two hours, a doctor enters the waiting room. Robin is asleep in the chair beside me.

"The medication is working," he says with a relieved smile. "The swelling is starting to go down, and he's beginning to stabilize."

I'm incredibly thankful to hear those words. "Thank you so much."

Robin wakes up, and I fill her in on the news.

"If you hadn't told Dr. Embrun about his allergy when you did, Wallace would have died. We're so grateful that you remembered that vital information." He puts a comforting hand on my shoulder. "It should be safe for you to go home for the night. We'll give you a call once he's fully stabilized." He gives me and Robin a polite smile.

As he walks away, Robin turns to me. "Oh my God Gen, you saved his life!" She hugs me.

Although we're not out of the woods yet, I feel so relieved.

Chapter 34

At around 4:00 a.m., I'm woken by a call from the hospital with an update on Wallace's condition.

"Your husband still has swelling on his brain. It's gone down significantly, but we aren't able to get it to where we want it to be," the doctor says. We're placing him into a medically induced coma to help the swelling go down fully and also to help minimize the damage to his frontal lobe."

"Damage? His frontal lobe is damaged? What does that mean?" I ask, worried.

"The frontal lobe is the front part of the brain. We'll explain in more detail when you come back in. On the latest scans, it appears that the swelling has caused a significant amount of damage to the front of his brain. We have to place him into a coma to limit as much trauma to his brain as possible. Do we have your consent to proceed?" I can barely process everything he's telling me.

"Of course. Anything to save him," I reply.

"Thank you, Mrs. Browne. Could you come back to the hospital around 8:00 a.m.? Dr. Embrun should be available to speak with you, accompanied by a neurologist, to discuss the next steps."

"Yes, of course."

When I hang up, my head is spinning. Brain damage? That sounds bad. I'm unable to go back to sleep, so I toss and turn in bed for what feels like hours.

"Mommy?" a young voice whispers. Maya is standing at my bedroom door, holding her blanket, which is dragging on the floor behind her.

"Why are you awake, baby?" I ask.

"I'm scared, Mommy. When is Daddy coming home?" she says in her baby voice while approaching the bed. I take her in my arms and lay her down next to me.

"I don't know. Hopefully soon." She clings onto me and rests her head on my chest. I stroke her hair with my fingers.

"Is he going to be okay?"

"I hope so, sweetheart. You need to go back to sleep. Everything will be okay." I wish I could believe my own words. In truth, I have no idea if he'll be okay. Yes, I know he'll likely survive, but the uncertainty of the situation worries me.

I lie there awake with Maya sleeping on my chest for over two hours. After I lose all feeling in my right arm, I slide out from under her and carry her back into bed. Lance and Alaina are still asleep.

I walk downstairs to make a cup of coffee, and I take a moment to sit at the dining table. My eyes are stinging and puffy from crying so much yesterday. Robin agreed to come over with the kids again today while I go back to the hospital and meet with the doctors. She's supposed to arrive at around 7:30 a.m.

I call my father to update him on Wallace's condition. Then I head upstairs to take a shower. As I look at my reflection in the mirror, tears escape my eyes. This version of me looks rundown, exhausted, and terrified. Out of all the things that happened in my life, I never would have predicted this. Wallace was doing so well, and so was our family. We were finally starting to live a comfortable life. Now I feel like we're about to lose everything we've worked so hard for.

I turn away from the mirror and get undressed. I stay in the shower for at least twenty minutes, trying to escape all the negative thoughts entering my mind.

...

I arrive at the hospital at exactly 8:00 a.m. Dr. Embrun is waiting for me with his colleague.

"This is Dr. Hosh," he says, "and he's the neurologist who's helping us treat your husband."

"It's nice to meet you, Mrs. Browne," Dr. Hosh says, shaking my hand and giving me a friendly smile.

"Please, if you could both just call me Genevieve," I say.

"Very well," Dr. Embrun replies. "If you could please follow us to my office, Genevieve."

Once we're seated in his office, me on one side of the desk and the doctors on the other, I ask when I can see Wallace.

"As soon as we're done here," Dr. Embrun replies.

"How is he doing?" I ask, looking at both of them.

"Well, from a physical standpoint, we expect Wallace to make a full recovery," Dr. Hosh replies. "However, the degree of damage that he suffered to his frontal lobe can't be fully assessed until after he wakes up."

"Yes, we're hoping to keep him in a medically induced coma for about two weeks to ensure that there's no further damage," Dr. Embrun adds.

"So, how badly is this going to affect Wallace? Will he be able to speak? Eat? Walk?" I ask, my voice breaking. Tears stream down my face again, and it burns. I've wiped my face so many times in the last twenty-four hours that my cheeks are raw.

"He might need to relearn a few motor skills, yes, but he should be able to regain those kinds of abilities in a matter of days with physiotherapy," Dr. Embrun says. "What we're concerned about are the functions related to his frontal lobe, the part where he suffered the injury."

"The frontal lobe is the part of the brain that affects behaviour, personality, and social skills," Dr. Hosh explains. "After your husband wakes up, you might notice a change in his ability to reason and concentrate, among other things. His behaviour and personality might be altered. We won't know the extent of his injuries until he wakes up."

My heart sinks. I can't find the words to respond. I just sit there, feeling perplexed.

"We understand how hard this is for you, Genevieve," Dr. Embrun says. "If you need a moment, we can step out. Just come back into the hallway when you're ready to see your husband."

I nod and they head out, closing the door behind them.

As soon as they leave, I start sobbing into my hands.

Chapter 35

Two weeks have gone by since my conversation with Dr. Embrun and Dr. Hosh. After ten days, the swelling on Wallace's brain was completely gone. They kept him in a coma for a few days after that, and they finally stopped administering the drugs last night, so he can wake up. They told me it could take up to forty-eight hours before he actually wakes.

Robin and Daniel have been taking turns watching my children while I visit Wallace at the hospital a few hours each day. I also reached out to Michael and Victoria to inform them of everything that's been going on. They took my kids for a few sleepovers last week to help take a bit of stress off my shoulders. I've never been away from my kids this often, but I don't want to bring them with me to the hospital for fear of traumatizing them. They've been missing their father so much, and I haven't been able to find the words to explain that their daddy might act differently when he comes home. It's been especially difficult to try to keep it together while I'm around my kids. Alaina knows that something really bad has happened, but Lance and Maya are too young to understand what's going on. I know it's been troubling them to see me crying this much, so my siblings and I have been trying everything we can to keep them occupied. Because all of this is happening during the summer, they can't even go to school to escape what's going on at home. Regardless of the outcome, I'm going to place them in therapy to prevent this trauma from affecting them over the long term.

My family doctor prescribed me sleeping pills because I was unable to sleep for several days. Whenever I closed my eyes, I would picture Wallace in the same state he was in the night I brought him to the hospital. Everything that has happened to him continues to haunt me. The doctors were unable to explain how Wallace caught a virus that attacked his brain, and it's been eating me up inside. How could we be this unlucky?

Part of me is terrified of Wallace waking up. Of course, I want him to wake up, so he can get through physiotherapy and then hopefully we can return to a somewhat normal but altered life. However, the uncertainty of how bad the damage is worries me. I find comfort in knowing that after everything we've gone through so far, we've persevered.

I'm expecting him to be different. I've already seen him display so many different behaviours and characteristics while he went through mania and depression, that I'm certain I'll be able to manage this too. My love for him is so strong, I can't imagine an obstacle that we won't be able to overcome.

Chapter 36

I leave my house for the hospital. It's been twenty-four hours since they stopped the drugs to induce the coma, and Wallace still hasn't woken up. The kids are staying with Mike and Vic again, so I take Robin with me to the hospital. It's a Saturday, so Norman is at home with their girls.

When we arrive in Wallace's hospital room, I sit on one side of the bed, and Robin sits on the other. Moments later, a nurse enters. "Good morning, Genevieve. We've seen Wallace make lots of movements in the last few hours. He should wake up anytime now."

She gives a comforting smile, then she turns on the bag connected to his feeding tube. When she lifts the blanket to check his tube site, I notice how slim Wallace has gotten. His ribs are protruding from his chest, and his legs look stick thin. Seeing that sends chills down my spine. The nurse notices my reaction.

"Don't worry," she says. "It appears worse because he lost some of his muscle mass from being completely immobile over the last two weeks. Once he gets up and starts moving, it won't take long for him to fill out again."

He looks so fragile, like simply touching him will break a bone. I look away until she finishes cleaning his tube site. When she's finished, I look at Robin, and she appears just as disturbed as I feel.

"Oh my God, Gen. It's really scary to see this up close," she whispers, gesturing to all the tubes protruding from him.

"I know," I reply. "It's been an ongoing nightmare."

Just then, we notice Wallace's feet twitch, and his eyes flicker. My heart starts racing. Robin and I stare at him. Minutes later, his eyes open.

"I'll go get the doctor," Robin says, standing up.

"Wallace?" I say. I look into his eyes, and something makes my stomach turn. The way he stares back at me, it's as though he doesn't recognize me. I try to mask my uneasiness. "Wallace. Can you hear me?"

"Yes," he mumbles. His gaze is sharp and disturbed, his expression unreadable. He looks away.

The nurse comes in with Robin.

"Hi, Mr. Browne. I'm happy to see that you're awake," the nurse says. She raises the bed, so he's in more of a seated position. He looks around the room, appearing disoriented. The nurse turns to us. "It's going to take a few minutes for him to adjust. After being in a comatose state for over two weeks, his mind will need some time to comprehend what's going on."

About thirty minutes later, Dr. Hosh enters the room. "Good morning, Genevieve." He smiles and then looks at Wallace. "Hello, Wallace! Welcome back, my friend." His tone sounds like he's talking to a child. It feels condescending, but at the same time, I know they're just trying to ease Wallace into this unknown environment. They have way more experience with this kind of thing than I do, so I'm not one to judge.

"Can you tell me where you are, Wallace?" Dr. Hosh asks as he begins his examination. Wallace doesn't respond to his question. Dr. Hosh shines a small flashlight into Wallace's eyes.

"Ah, fuck!" Wallace yells, swiping Dr. Hosh's hand away from his face. The flashlight flies across the room. Wallace closes his eyes and rubs them with his fingers. Everyone's eyes widen in shock.

"I'm so sorry, Wallace," Dr. Hosh says as he picks up his flashlight. "I'll come back later when you're feeling better."

Dr. Hosh signals for me to follow him into the hallway.

"What just happened?" I ask.

"It isn't unusual for Wallace to have reacted that way. However, I would have thought that his eyes had adjusted to the fluorescent lights in the room by now. This little pen light isn't strong enough to cause such a strong negative reaction. Although he didn't address me directly, he's responsive, which is a good sign. It's normal for patients with traumatic brain injuries to act more aggressively or get easily agitated. Wallace's brain needs to adjust to the trauma it endured. Now that he's awake, I suggest you prepare yourself to witness personality and behavioural changes. He's the same person physically, but he'll never be the same as he was before his injury. You'll need to adjust your family's life accordingly."

When he notices tears rolling down my face again, he places his hand on my shoulder. "You'll be okay, Genevieve. You're strong. Your husband needs your support right now. He will feel lost at times. The brain doesn't know it's been injured. He may never recognize that he's changed. But I'm confident that you'll be able to navigate through it with him." He gives me a sympathetic look, then goes back into the room.

My back is against the wall, and I let my legs drop, sliding down to the floor. I place my face into my hands to muffle my cries.

Robin comes out of the room. When she sees me, she sits next to me and holds me tight. "It's going to be okay, Gen. It's going to get better," she says, trying to comfort me.

"How can it get better?" I ask, lifting my face from my hands. "I don't even recognize the man in there! In the eighteen years I've known him, I've never seen him react like that! Wallace has never shown any signs of violence. Never." I cry even harder.

"I know, honey. I know." Robin places my head against her chest and strokes my hair. She has nothing else to say, knowing that nothing she can say will reassure me.

When we return to Wallace's room, Dr. Hosh and a nurse are there, looking at Wallace's chart. "I just told Wallace that we're going to take him for some scans soon to get another look at his brain now that he's awake," Dr. Hosh says. Wallace is sitting on the bed, staring at the wall.

"We'll come back soon to get him ready." Dr. Hosh and the nurse walk out.

I turn to Robin. "Is it okay if I have a few minutes alone with him?" I ask.

"Of course, Gen. Dad and Daniel called me earlier to say they were on their way. I'll go into the lobby to wait for them. I have my phone on me. Call if you need anything."

"Sounds good. Thank you, Robin." She smiles at me, then walks out of the room. I take a seat next to Wallace's bed.

"Hi, Wallace. Why won't you look at me?" I ask. He doesn't answer. "How are you feeling?"

"Like shit. Everyone is treating me like a freak."

"No one is treating you like a freak, babe. You just went through hell. You almost died," I say, trying to reassure him.

"Stop fucking lying! I can see your face from the corner of my eye. You're looking at me like I'm crazy!"

I back away from him.

"Wallace, stop it. I've spent the last two and half weeks worried sick. I stayed with you every single day you've been in the hospital. I was terrified of losing you!"

He finally turns to me, his dark brown eyes, which I've been looking into for the last eighteen years, barely recognizable. His penetrating gaze instills fear in me. I feel a chill go up my spine. As he stares at me, a slight smirk forms on his lips, and his expression makes me uneasy. His features are the same as they've always been, other than being sunken from weight loss. However, something about him looks different. Before his accident, whenever I looked at him, he appeared soft, gentle, and kind. His eyes always displayed a look of affection and admiration toward me. Now they're filled with wrath and resentment. I take a deep breath, trying to hide my fear to avoid upsetting him.

"Something is different about you, Genevieve." He tilts his head and gives me a once-over. "I can tell that you resent me." His smirk turns into a frown, and he starts crying hysterically. I'm frozen in place, unsure how to react. The way his expression changed so quickly feels sinister. It's like all of the characteristics from his depressive and manic episodes have merged together, amplified by a thousand times. Before I can say anything else, my dad, Daniel, and Robin enter the room.

"What's wrong, Wallace?" Robin asks.

"Nothing. I'm sorry. I'm just so thankful to be alive," he says between sobs, his expression softening. My dad and Robin stand next to him at the bed, rubbing his back to comfort him as he cries.

I sit there, dumbfounded and unable to process what just happened.

All I can think is, *What... the... fuck?*

Chapter 37

It's been six weeks since Wallace woke up, and he's finally ready to be discharged from the hospital. He had to relearn how to walk and swallow by himself. He has received extensive physical therapy for almost a month, and he's already regained all of his motor functions. Dr. Hosh has been monitoring him closely, and although Wallace is not yet cleared to drive, Dr. Hosh thinks he's been recovering at an outstanding rate. The damage to his frontal lobe was slightly less severe than what they anticipated, and they think he should be able to return to normal activities after a few months. He's also been assigned to a new psychiatrist who specializes in brain injuries. He's been assessing Wallace regularly to ensure he's adjusting to the way his mind now functions. He's going to need therapy to help him through the trauma he experienced.

Since the first day he woke up, he hasn't shown any signs of violence or malevolent behaviour. It's been messing with my mind because I've been feeling on edge the entire time, waiting for a new, eerie side of him to creep out again. I was worried about bringing the kids to see him, but when I finally did, he showed nothing but joy and excitement.

He's kind and respectful toward others. He becomes slightly agitated whenever we talk too loudly or when he feels overstimulated, but otherwise he's doing well.

Despite this behaviour, there's still something off when I look at him. His expression is different. I don't know if that's due to the brain injury, but I have a bad feeling about it. I've tried explaining it to my family, but they don't see what I'm seeing. I wish I could pinpoint exactly what's different about him.

"We're going to start with three sessions per week, then we'll adjust according to your progress," Wallace's new psychiatrist, Dr. Evians, says. "I want to meet with you once a week as well, Genevieve," he adds, handing me one of his business cards. After everything Wallace had gone through, I haven't been able to return to work. The school board requires me to be assessed by a psychiatrist for them to pay for my leave. Everything that's happened has been traumatic for me as well. Since Wallace can't work or drive for the next few months, it's better for me to stay with him and ensure that he's okay while at home. Alaina and Lance have returned to school, but Maya is only three, and she's still staying at home with us. I don't know if I trust Wallace yet to take care of her alone, and I can't rely on my family and friends to take over all the time since they have their own busy lives.

I thank Dr. Evians, then I take Maya's hand and walk back into the hallway. Wallace is right behind us.

Dr. Embrun sees us standing there and approaches us. "Going home at last, are we?" He looks at Wallace and me, a big smile on his face.

"Yes. I can't wait to sleep in my own bed," Wallace says.

"I can imagine. Are you excited that Daddy is coming home, Maya?" Dr. Embrun asks, crouching to her level.

"Yes!" Maya says. He laughs and then stands up.

"I wish luck and health to you all," he says, then he gives me a hug. "If you ever need anything, call me," he whispers in my ear.

"Thank you for everything, Dr. Embrun," I reply, smiling. "You and Dr. Hosh have really helped us through this."

"It was our pleasure. We're happy to see our wonderful patient here bouncing back so gracefully." He taps Wallace's shoulder.

Wallace smiles. "I couldn't have done it without either of you."

"Alright. Well, I won't keep you any longer. I'm sure you must be eager to get out of here."

We thank him one last time, then head toward the elevators.

"I'm so happy you're coming home," I say to Wallace.

"Me too, babe. Me too." He leans over and kisses me on the lips. "I've been wishing for this day since I woke up."

I feel a pit in my stomach after he says those words. Flashbacks of that day come rushing into my mind. I hold Maya's hand tighter. A big part of me worries that he will show that side again and that it will happen soon.

We arrive at home just past 2:30 p.m., right before Alaina and Lance get home from school. Maya fell asleep in the car, so I lay her in her bed and shut her bedroom door. When I walk back downstairs, Wallace is standing at the foot of the steps.

"What time are Alaina and Lance coming home from school?" he asks.

"Not for another hour," I reply.

Wallace takes me up into his arms and twirls me around. "God, I've missed you," he says, kissing me. I pull away slightly, my arms still wrapped around his neck.

"What about the kids?" I ask, giggling. "I have to get dinner started."

"You just said we have an hour. Maya's sleeping. Let's take the kids out to eat later, so we can celebrate," he whispers in my ear and then kisses my neck. My heart flutters from his touch, and goosebumps form on my skin as he traces his fingers up and down my back. I've missed him so much over the last several weeks.

"Okay, yes. Let's celebrate," I reply, unable to focus on anything other than the feeling of his lips tracing down my collarbone.

Chapter 38

We have a pleasant night as a family. We take the kids to our favourite Italian restaurant, and they love it. Alaina and Lance are so happy to have their father back home. We put all three kids to bed by 11:00 p.m., so Wallace and I can watch a movie together. It feels like a typical Friday night like we used to have before he got sick.

As I cuddle up to him, he points the remote control at the TV and tries to turn it on, but it doesn't work. He takes the batteries out and then replaces them, but it still won't work.

"Shit," he mumbles. "Where are those batteries I bought a few months ago?"

"I'm not sure. Let me go look." I go to get up, but he tells me to sit, then he rummages through the drawers in the kitchen. "Where the hell are they?" he shouts. I jump up and run to the kitchen.

"Babe, calm down," I whisper. "You're going to wake the kids."

"I know I put them here. I remember doing it. Where did you put them?" he asks, growing more agitated.

"I don't know, honey. That was three months ago. They could have been misplaced by me or the kids."

"If you would actually discipline the brats instead of letting them do whatever the fuck they want, they wouldn't hide the things that I've bought!" His eyes are filled with rage, the same darkness I saw in his eyes the first time he woke up.

I step back, frightened of him. I can't believe the words that just came out of his mouth.

"You don't mean that! You know how hard we've worked to raise polite, respectful kids. That has nothing to do with these misplaced batteries. How dare you say that about me and them?" I try not to raise my voice too much.

When he sees the tears spilling from my eyes, his shoulders drop, and he calms down, his rage turning to regret.

"I'm so sorry," he whispers. "I don't know why I said that. I'm so sorry." His eyes fill with tears. "It's just hard to control my anger lately. I'm sorry. I'm trying." He lowers his head.

We stand in silence. I try to calm myself down before I speak. "I know it's hard, Wallace. It's okay."

He starts crying uncontrollably. I get closer and embrace him. He wraps his arms around me, his shoulders shaking as he tries to calm down. "And the tears," he says, "They just come. I can't stop them. I hate how I can't control myself. Why is this happening to me?"

"Shh. Babe, don't worry. It will be okay," I say, still feeling on edge. I can't wrap my head around what just happened. I'm worried about how such a little thing ticked him off. I can't imagine him reacting this way if one of the kids does something that upsets him. During the six weeks he stayed at the hospital, he didn't lash out once. Not with the doctors, not with my family, not with the kids, and not with me. I don't understand why he's unable to control himself now that he's out. I feel like I've allowed a stranger into my home.

After he calms down, we manage to find the batteries for the remote and watch a movie together. I'm not as affectionate as I was before the incident. I feel hesitant, not knowing how to behave so he doesn't get angry again.

After the movie, we head upstairs to get ready for bed. He rushes to use the bathroom before me. Before he got sick, I always used the bathroom first. We've done it that way for years. He always prioritized my needs. I'm a bit put off, then I tell myself I'm overreacting. It's his first night home, and he hasn't had a chance to adjust to a routine. It's no big deal. I just feel that the Wallace I know wouldn't overlook a small detail like that. He knows how important little things are. It makes me sad to know this is probably one of the behavioural changes that come with his brain injury.

After we're done with the bathroom, I turn off the lights and slip into bed next to him. I contemplate taking a sleeping pill, then I decide against it. I know I won't get any quality sleep tonight, not until I go through at least one night with him. He kisses me on the forehead and then rolls over and falls asleep. I close my eyes and try to think of nice things. Maybe it'll get better the more he gets used to being back home. Maybe his psychiatrist will convince him to go back on his medication, or maybe the therapy will help. Either way, things will get better. They have to.

...

I wake up in the middle of the night, and I can't breathe. I try to scream, but it's muffled by whatever is pushing down on my face. I realize it's a pillow, and I use all of my strength to push it off me. The pressure releases, and I gasp for air. The pillow is lifted off my face, revealing Wallace on top of me.

"What the fuck are you doing?" I yell. "You're trying to kill me!"

I throw him off of me and jump off the bed, heading toward the corner of the room.

"You were snoring," he says. "It was disrupting my sleep. I just wanted to sleep peacefully. I wasn't going to kill you." He shrugs as if he didn't just traumatize me.

He lies back down on his side of the bed and turns the other way. Moments later, I hear him snoring. What a hypocrite.

I go into the girls' bedroom and lie down next to Maya, facing the bedroom door. Then I check the time on the alarm clock: 1:56 a.m.

There's no way I can go back to sleep after what he just did. I lie there unable to close my eyes for fear that he will barge into the room.

It's going to be a long night.

Chapter 39

It's been a month since Wallace came home, and I feel trapped in my own house. He's like a ticking bomb, and I'm just waiting for the next time he's going to explode. I haven't slept much in the last several weeks because I'm so afraid that he'll do something to me in my sleep. Since that night when he tried suffocating me with a pillow, he's been constantly getting agitated with me, like he can't stand being in the same room with me. On the other hand, whenever it's time for bed, he becomes fixated on wanting to be intimate with me in a way that's excessive and abnormal. If I refuse, he starts acting aggressively, so I feel like I have to give in or else he'll do something to hurt me. I never thought I would feel this way toward my own husband, but I'm terrified of him.

I've taken the kids with me over to my father's house a few nights per week, so we can get some time away from him. Even the children are starting to be afraid of Wallace.

For the first few days, he tried to control himself around them, but then one night, he blew up at Maya because she was crying. If I hadn't been there to intervene, he would have hit her hard enough to make her bleed. He can barely stand our children's presence ever since. He's also been acting violent and malicious but in a way that I couldn't prove if I called the police on him. He screams in my face, threatening to hurt me, but so far he hasn't. But he does do things to torment the kids and me. He turned off the hot water for the shower, then broke the boiler handle, and he's left the front door wide open in the middle of the night more than once, allowing anyone or anything to come inside while we're asleep. We even woke up one morning to find all the food in the house was gone. He emptied the cabinets and the fridge, then left with my purse, so I had no way of getting food without calling someone. I don't understand why he's going out of his way to hurt me when I've done nothing but try to help him.

Lately, he's been leaving the house for days at a time without telling me where he's going. It worries me because I have no idea what he does when he's gone. He could be getting into trouble. I'm afraid of what he's capable of, so it makes me incredibly anxious whenever I can't be around to try to control his behaviour. Just yesterday he was gone all day and night and he didn't come back to the house until 4:00 a.m., and I have no idea where he went. He took a taxi somewhere and refused to tell me anything. I can't know for sure, but I'm certain he's cheating on me. He's come home smelling like another woman's perfume, but I'm too afraid of what he's going to do to me if I try to confront him.

I can't believe this is the man that I married. Wallace used to be kind, empathetic, and loving. It's as if he's been replaced by a complete maniac.

I'm struggling to find the man I love in the person who now sleeps next to me.

Wallace is sitting with me at the dining table drinking a cup of coffee while Maya is in the living room, watching a cartoon.

"Mike is coming to visit while I go to therapy," I tell him. "He said he wanted to see you now that you're back home." I avoid looking directly at him.

"Mike is a fucking back stabber," he replies.

"What?"

"This whole time, he's been trying to get with you. Why do you think he wanted to hang out with us all the time? He wants to be with you, and he's just pretending to be my friend. I don't want him here."

"Wallace, that's not true. Michael and Victoria have been our good friends for years. He's never looked at me in the way that you're implying."

"He's constantly flirting with you. You're just too much of an airhead to see it." His comment makes me angry. I hate when he acts irrational.

"Can you stop insulting me please? He's coming to see you; he's already on his way. Can I trust that you'll remain civil with him while I'm gone? Or should I reschedule my appointment?"

"Go. I'll be fine."

I let out a huge sigh. "Maya's coming with me. I don't want her to be caught in the middle if you end up fighting with him."

He doesn't reply.

I pick Maya up and head to the entrance to get our coats and shoes on. It's the middle of November, so it's already quite cold outside. I put Maya's pink sparkly hat on. It matches her jacket.

When I open the door, Michael is already standing on the porch.

"Hi, Mike," I whisper, then motion for him to walk outside with me.

"Hey, Gen. How are you guys doing?" he asks.

"Not great," I reply. I've told him and Vic everything that's going on with Wallace, including the outbursts, the extreme mood changes, and the violent behaviour. They could barely believe that I was speaking about my husband when I described all the things he's done since he came home. They've been hesitant to visit, but Micheal decided to see for himself what I was dealing with.

"When I told him you were coming, he started accusing you of trying to take me from him. He might try to start a fight with you. It may be wise to just let him be and come back another time. I don't want something bad to happen."

He pauses to think. "I'm sure it'll be fine, Gen. If he gets violent, I'll call the police. I want to know what you've been going through these last few weeks. And I want to make sure that you have a witness if, God forbid, you ever need one."

"Thanks, Mike. I really appreciate it," I reply, smiling. He smiles back and then heads into the house.

On the way to my appointment, I call my dad to see if he can watch Maya while I'm in therapy.

"Mike was supposed to stay with her and Wallace," I explain, "but Wallace is acting strange toward Mike, and I'm worried that it isn't safe there for Maya."

"Of course," he replies. "I'm on my way home from the supermarket. I'll be there by the time you arrive."

When I park in the driveway of my dad's house, I notice an unfamiliar car parked beside me. If my dad got a new car, I'm sure he would've placed it in the garage instead of parking it outside. I take Maya out of her car seat and head inside the house.

"Grandpa!" Maya shouts in excitement, then runs into my dad's arms.

"Hi, my sweet girl. Are you excited to spend some time with your old granddad?" he says as he kisses her on the cheek.

"Thanks so much for watching her, Dad," I say, giving him a hug and a kiss.

"Anything for you, my baby," he replies. "I'm so sorry for everything you're going through, hon. However, I think I might have someone here who'll cheer you up. I ran into him while I was at the store."

He walks me into the living room, and sitting on the couch is Ramon!

Chapter 40

"Ramon? Oh my God, it's been years!"

He gets up from the sofa and runs up to me, giving me a hug. "It's been way too long, Gen. Way too long." He hugs me tighter.

"What are you doing here?" I ask, pulling away. Ramon and I have barely kept in touch over the last decade. When he moved to Vancouver after my wedding, it made it difficult for us to communicate, since long-distance calls were expensive. We would send each other letters every so often, but we never had the chance to catch up. The last time I saw him was when he flew in for my mother's funeral, but he was only able to stay for a couple of days.

"My father passed away a few days ago. I came to town for his funeral." With everything going on in my life, I hadn't heard the news of his father passing.

"I'm so sorry, Ramon. My condolences." I give him another hug.

"Thank you, Gen," he replies.

"I have an appointment that I have to get to, but I'd love to catch up with you," I say. "How long are you staying in town?"

"Two weeks." He smiles. "I'd really like that."

"I'll watch Maya for a little longer if you want to grab a coffee with Ramon after your appointment, sweetheart," my father says.

"Thanks, Dad. But I'm not sure how long Mike is staying with Wallace. I should probably head straight home." I look at Ramon. "But maybe sometime this week?"

"Yeah. I'll call you, and we'll plan something," he says.

Ramon has no idea what's happened to Wallace, but I have a feeling my dad is going to catch him up on everything while I'm gone.

I arrive at Dr. Evians' office. I was supposed to have my first session with him over three weeks ago, but he's been overbooked. He considers Wallace to be a higher priority than me. After he hears what I've been going through, I'm sure I'll rise higher up his priority list.

I look at my watch. It's 10:03 a.m. Dr. Evians has never been late for any of Wallace's sessions, so I'm hoping mine wasn't cancelled without me knowing. I've been bringing Wallace to each of his sessions, and Maya has been coming with us while the other two are at school. I'm surprised he agrees to go, especially considering the way he's been behaving. He probably puts on an act during his sessions with Dr. Evians to hide who he has become.

That's what I'm hoping to discuss during my session today, so I can finally get some professional advice. As much as I've loved Wallace for all these years, I can't go on like this, and I need someone to validate my need to leave him. That way I can finally gain the courage to do it.

"Genevieve? You can come in now," Dr. Evians says.

I follow him into his office.

"Take a seat, Genevieve. I want you to tell me how you've been doing since Wallace has come back home."

I tell him everything, from the first time I was alone with Wallace after he woke up in the hospital to his most recent outburst. I tell him how unsafe I feel in my home with him there, and I tell him how I don't know how long I can stay with him if he continues to behave this way. Dr. Evians doesn't seem surprised at my revelation.

"Interesting," he replies as he makes notes. "Well, Genevieve, you were informed that Wallace was going to experience some behavioural and personality changes. This is something that you and your family will have to adapt to."

What?

"Yes, I know. But this is absurd. No one can live this way. I understand that he's changed, but it's not just that; he's become violent. I fear that my kids and I might be in danger." I try not to get too upset, but I don't get how he's taking Wallace's side after what I just revealed to him. He's basically telling me this is how things are going to be from now on and that I should accept it.

"You have to understand that Wallace also suffers from bipolar disorder," Dr. Evians says. "This can amplify the traits of someone who suffers a frontal-lobe injury. The good thing is, he seems to be responding well to therapy. It's only been a month, Genevieve. I suggest you give him a bit more time. I'm hoping we can work toward getting him back on his medication to treat his mental illness. Doing that should help with his violent outbursts and irritability." I don't think he understands that it's much more than just "irritability."

"He told me he would never go back on those meds," I reply. "I've already suggested that to him. He said he would rather kill himself than feel the effects of that medication again." I start crying. I feel desperate for support, but I'm not getting any from Dr. Evians.

"Genevieve, he won't change overnight. Progress isn't linear. It's going to take time, but we can work on managing his behaviour. However, to succeed in doing that, he needs your support. You can't give up on him now."

I feel like I've been told "you can't give up on him" way too many times in the last eighteen years. I've been through everything with Wallace. I've loved him through the darkness, the light, the highs, and the lows. I've been through it all. I've supported him through the most difficult times of his life, but there is only so much I can give. What happens when I'm the one who needs support? I never thought I would reach a breaking point. I never thought I would feel this way, but I just can't do it anymore.

"You don't understand, Dr. Evians," I say, sobbing. "He's never going to be the same. I lost my husband the day he was brought into the hospital. I can't go on like this." My voice breaks. Dr. Evians just stares at me with a blank look.

"Genevieve, listen to me. You have to remember your marriage vows. You can't leave him. You can't do this to your marriage," he says with a hint of annoyance in his tone.

I look at him in disbelief—and anger. "You have some nerve," I say, wiping my tears away with the sleeve of my jacket. "I have more than just my marriage to think about! My children are involved! I can't keep putting them through this. They deserve a better life than this. *I* deserve a better life than this! How dare you remind *me* of my marriage vows when *he's* the one who broke every single one of them! Try living with this man for even a week. I bet you couldn't last a day! He puts on a nice front with you during your one-hour sessions, but he's horrible to me and my children. He's manipulative, violent, and *evil.* I know he's the one who suffered a brain injury. I know he's the one who's sick. But how far will you go before you stop using that as an excuse for his malevolent behaviour? Are you going to wait for him to kill my children and me? How can you neglect our safety in favour of his needs? You're minimizing the severity of the situation, and you don't care what happens to my children or me as long as he's taken care of. How fucked up is that?"

I laugh at how ridiculous it all feels. This is the moment I realize I have no support from this doctor or any other mental health professional as long as I'm not the one who's suffering from a psychiatric disorder. The system is broken, and I'm utterly alone in fighting against the man who makes me fear for my life.

"I understand how upsetting this must feel—"

I storm out of the room before he can finish his sentence.

Once I'm in my car, I scream at the top of my lungs and pound the steering wheel until I'm out of breath. I look at myself in the rearview mirror. Then I fix my hair and wipe off the mascara that's running down my face. *I need to stay strong.*

I pull myself together as best as I can, then I drive back to my dad's house to pick up Maya.

When I arrive, I notice that Ramon's car is still in the driveway. Inside, my dad and Ramon are sitting at the dining table. Maya is on the couch, looking at a book.

"Oh, my sweet baby, what happened?" my dad asks as he gets up and gives me a hug. I sob into his chest.

"I can't do this anymore, Daddy," I say between cries.

Ramon gets up and stands behind me, rubbing my back. "I'm so sorry, Gen," he says.

I lift my head from my dad's chest, and he wipes the tears from my face with his thumbs. The last thing I want right now is to go back home.

"Do you think we could actually go for that coffee now?" I ask Ramon.

"Of course," he says, and my father gives an approving nod.

Chapter 41

Ramon and I go to a local coffee shop, and I spend the next hour telling him about everything I've been through from the moment Wallace stopped taking his medication after Lance was born, to the encounter I just had with Dr. Evians. I've cried so much already this morning that tears can no longer form in my eyes as I recall every traumatic event from the last five years. Ramon is speechless, unable to believe what I'm revealing to him.

"You have to leave him, Gen," he says when I'm finished. "There must be someone who can help you. What about Dr. Hosh or Dr. Embrun? I'm sure one of them can provide some kind of support."

"I can't go through that again, Ramon. Evians basically told me to suck it up. I know he thinks I'm exaggerating Wallace's behaviour. Wallace controls himself around everyone but me! It's like he wants to convince people that I'm the one who's crazy!" When I say that, it hits me that I haven't called Mike to check in on him.

"Here, I'll prove it," I tell Ramon. I dial Mike's phone number and put my phone on speaker mode.

"Hello? Gen?" Mike says.

"Hey, Mike, are you still with Wallace?"

"No. I left after fifteen minutes. He said his sister was coming to pick him up."

Candace?

"How was he with you?" I ask, intrigued. Ramon is listening attentively.

"He was fine. He was acting slightly odd, but he didn't mention anything you told me before you left. He did make me feel uneasy, though. He was acting nice, but it felt exaggerated and insincere. And he had a creepy look in his eye. I don't know, Gen. I think something's really wrong with him."

He's the first person who has been able to describe something similar to what I noticed with Wallace since the moment he woke up in the hospital.

"After everything you've told me, and after what I've seen in just fifteen minutes of speaking with him, I don't think it's safe for you to be alone with him and the kids. I have a feeling that he might harm you or your kids the next chance that he gets. I don't want to alarm you, but I think he's dangerous. I have a weird feeling that he's waiting for the right time to do something horrible." His words give me goosebumps. It's like he's confirming what I've been too afraid to say out loud.

Ramon looks at me with concern. "What does Candace's car look like?" he asks.

"I haven't seen her in years. Last time I saw her, she had an old blue sedan. But she could be driving anything now. Why do you ask?"

"Did it look anything like that?" He points into the distance. Our table is in front of a large window facing the parking lot, and there's a blue sedan parked a few spots from where we're seated. That car looks like the same one Candace used to drive.

"Oh my God, it does! Did they follow us here?"

They must have realized we spotted them because the car speeds out of the parking lot.

My phone rings. It's an unknown number. I look at Ramon, and he motions for me to answer it.

"You lying, cheating bitch! You'll pay for this, you fucking whore." The line goes dead.

Neither of us recognize the voice, but it must be Wallace. My heart starts racing, and I try not to have a panic attack, but I feel like I can't breathe.

Noticing my panicked state, Ramon leans across the table and places his hands on mine. "Genevieve, you need to breathe. You can't go back home. We need to pick up Maya at your dad's and then get Alaina and Lance from school. You need to warn everyone that Wallace might show up at their house looking for you. You and the kids are going to stay with me in my hotel room. There are two separate beds and a cot. It'll be okay."

I'm shaking uncontrollably, I've never felt so terrified.

"What if he finds my car?" I ask.

"We'll drop off your car at home. I think they followed us here, so now they know what mine looks like. There's a car that belonged to my dad stored in the garage at his house. We'll switch vehicles before picking up Alaina and Lance, then head to the hotel."

On the way to my dad's house, I call Robin to let her know what's going on. She suggests that Dad stay with her until things calm down. After that I call Victoria and then Daniel to make them aware of the situation. Meanwhile, Robin calls Dad.

When we get to his house, he has his bags packed and is waiting at the door with Maya in his arms. He follows us to Robin's house. There's no sign of Candace's car anywhere, so I don't think that she and Wallace are still following us.

After we drop off Dad, we drive back to my house to leave my car there. Before we leave, I check multiple times to ensure that no one is following us.

Once we get to Ramon's father's house, we swap cars, then go to Alaina and Lance's school to go pick them up. On the way, I call the school to let them know I'll be taking the kids out early. Alaina and Lance attend the school that I teach at. My colleagues are somewhat aware of the situation. I had to disclose to the principal what was going on when I went on sick leave, and she told all the other teachers in the school. They know Wallace was in a coma due to a traumatic brain injury, but I don't think they're aware of anything else. I no longer work in the same school as Mike and Vic, and since starting at this school two years ago, I haven't had the chance to become friends with any of my colleagues, so there's no opportunity for anyone to find out the details of what's going on.

I hope that when we arrive, no one sees me in the car with Ramon. I don't want any gossip going around the school that I've been seen with a man other than my husband. I don't want any rumours to spread, not only for my own reputation but also for my children's sake. Alaina and Lance are already going through enough with what's happening with their father. They don't need anyone at school accusing their mom of cheating. School is probably the only place right now where they can escape all the problems we have at home. It breaks my heart that my children are being put through this, and I pray it will get better soon. Once I officially leave Wallace, we'll be able to move on from all the pain and suffering he has caused us over the past month.

When we arrive, I tell Ramon to wait in the car with Maya while I get the kids. The principal, Freida, who is also my boss, greets me at the front desk.

"Genevieve, it's so lovely to see you!" she says. "How are you and your husband doing? I heard he's been back home for a month now."

I contemplate whether or not I should tell her the truth. She reached out to me when I applied for sick leave, but she hasn't checked on me since. I can feel the insincerity in her voice when she speaks to me.

"Honestly, Freida, things aren't going well. I'm going to have a follow up in a few weeks with HR regarding my leave, but I don't think I'll be coming back at all this year."

"Oh dear, I'm so sorry to hear that, Genevieve. Don't you think it would be healthier for you to return to work, so you can have an escape from home?" It's comical how tone deaf she sounds. If only she knew what I was going through. I can only imagine what her and the other teachers say about me while I'm not there to defend myself.

"I wish I could, Freida. Unfortunately, with my husband almost dying and then coming back from his coma as a complete psychopath, it's a little difficult to focus on work right now. But thanks so much for the suggestion!"

She looks offended by my mockery. "I know what you're going through, you know! My husband suffered a brain injury after falling at work. Lord knows it was hard, but we got through it! You just have to adjust; that's all. I had to remember that it was not his fault that he changed and that he was still worthy of love. I wouldn't go as far as to call him a psychopath, though. That's low of you, Genevieve, speaking of your husband in that way." The audacity for her to compare her situation to mine in an attempt to show that she's much better than me at handling this kind of situation. I do everything in my power not to blow up on her.

"You have *no* idea what I've been through, Freida, and you have no idea what you're talking about. Switch places with me for a day, and you'll eat your words." She's too stunned to respond. "I'm pulling my kids out of school for the rest of the week. I'll let you know when they're ready to come back."

I see Alaina and Lance, holding hands as they walk down the hallway. I direct them out the door without looking back at Freida.

I'm worried that I may have just lost my job, but too much is happening right now for me to care. I just want to make sure my babies are safe.

"Mommy, what's going on?" Alaina asks. She and Lance are sitting on either side of Maya in the backseat. She sounds frightened. She's the only one of my three children who knows what's going on with Wallace. The other two are still too young to understand why he's acting so strange.

"We're going to stay in a hotel tonight. Something came up, so Daddy won't be able to join us." I try to hide the reality of the situation as best as I can, but I know it won't be long before they learn the truth.

"Mommy, who is this man?" Lance asks, puzzled. Even in a situation like this, Lance can still make me laugh with his frankness.

"This is my friend, Ramon. He's going to be staying with us at the hotel. Ramon and I have been friends since high school, and he's a kind man. I think you'll like him."

Ramon takes his eyes off the road for a second to smile at me. For the first time in what feels like forever, I sense comfort and security while looking at him. I realize how much I've missed having someone like him in my life.

"Okay. Can Ramon play dinosaurs with me then?" Lance asks. "Daddy hasn't played with me since he got back from the hospital." Lance has been fixated on dinosaurs ever since Wallace brought him to a dinosaur exhibition when he was three years old. It breaks my heart that he may no longer share that bond with his father.

"I would be honoured to play dinosaurs with you, Lance. But you'll have to show me how it's done since you're the expert," Ramon says. Lance's eyes light up.

"Deal!" he says. I look back at Alaina, who is staring at her feet, probably wondering what's going on. I nudge her shoulder to get her attention, and she looks at me.

"It's going to be okay, baby. Something is happening with Daddy, and we need to stay away from him for a bit. I don't want you to worry, and I won't let anything bad happen to you." I try to give her a reassuring smile, but I'm not sure she buys it. She just nods and then lowers her head again. I sigh and turn back around. Ramon places his hand on mine, but I pull away from his touch, knowing Alaina will misinterpret the gesture, and I don't want to upset her even more.

"I know you did that to comfort me," I whisper to Ramon. "But they won't understand."

He nods in agreement. "I'm sorry. I wasn't thinking."

"It's okay. I appreciate it," I reply, smiling.

Chapter 42

It's after 10:00 p.m., and the kids are asleep. They've had a long day, but we managed to keep their minds busy in the hotel room. Ramon went out and bought some board games. He even found one with a dinosaur theme. We spent the day playing and then we watched a movie and ate snacks before putting the kids to bed. Alaina and Maya are sleeping in one bed, and Lance and I are in the other. Ramon insisted on taking the cot.

Ramon gets out of the washroom after taking a shower. I showered before him, so I'm already lying in bed. I didn't take the time to bring a change of clothes for myself or the kids. The kids were wearing comfortable clothes already, so they are going to sleep in that. I borrowed a shirt and sweatpants from Ramon to sleep in since I was wearing jeans with an uncomfortable blouse all day. It feels nice to change into something comfortable after such a crazy day.

"Do you want to have some leftover pizza on the balcony?" Ramon asks as he towels his hair dry. "You've barely eaten all day. You must be so hungry." His shirt lifts up a bit with his arms, and it's the first time I notice his physique. He looks fit. I turn away from him after I realize what's on my mind. "Yeah, that would be nice," I say, blushing slightly but hoping he didn't notice me checking him out.

As Ramon heats up the pizza in the microwave, I head out the balcony and sit near the little round table in the corner. Ramon joins me soon after and places the pizza box in front of me.

"Thank you," I say, smiling at him.

"Of course. It was nothing. Just sixty seconds in the microwave."

"I mean, thank you for everything you've done for me today. You have no idea how much I appreciate it." I look into his dark blue eyes and watch them brighten.

"I haven't forgotten what I told you on your wedding night, Genny," he says. I haven't forgotten either. "I told you that if anything ever changed between you and Wallace that I would support and care for you. I can't say I'm happy I've had to carry out that promise because of what that entails. But I'm so happy that after all these years, you still trust me enough to allow me to protect you and your children. It's an honour, Genny. I'm beyond grateful that I showed up when I did. It makes me believe that everything happens for a reason."

I smile again, especially after his last sentence. It reminds me of what I told myself after giving birth to Maya.

"Thank you so much, Ramon. I don't know what I would do without you. You came like a blessing from the sky today. Tell me about your life, Ramon. Tell me about what you've been up to all these years. I'm sorry I haven't given you the chance before now, but I'm dying to know."

"It's a lot less exciting than your life; that's for sure." He laughs. I reach across the table to hit him playfully in the shoulder.

"I would rather have anything other than this kind of 'excitement.'"

"Seriously, I've been doing well. I haven't been home much since I moved out west because I've been busy. After landing that job in software engineering, I became friends with this guy who was planning to become certified in cybersecurity. He wanted me to join him, and after learning more about it, I realized how much it interested me. After we got our certifications, we worked as cybersecurity engineers for over six years. We ended up designing and building an efficient home security system. Two years later, we started our own company to sell the system. That accomplishment has been more rewarding than I could have ever dreamed of. However, it cost me time with my family and my friends back home." He looks down. "When I heard that my dad passed away, I hadn't seen him in over a year, and it hurts me so much. I should have been there for him in his last moments, you know?" Ramon's voice breaks, and tears form in his eyes. "I tried so hard to make him proud, but I was barely around to enjoy it with him."

"I'm so sorry, Ramon. I'm sure he knew how much you loved him." I move my chair to his side of the table and take his hand in mine to comfort him, placing my head on his shoulder.

"He tried so hard to support me when we lost Mom. He tried so hard to be there for me, but he couldn't get past his own grief. I hate to admit it, but he felt like a burden to me when I was in school. He had unwittingly put every responsibility onto me, and I resented him for it. I was so desperate to escape that I chose the farthest job possible, so I could get away from that feeling. I love the life I have out there, but I've missed out on so much here. Now, all these years later, I'm left grieving him all alone. Just like he did when I left."

By then he's sobbing. I put my arms around him, tears falling down my cheeks as well. I'm heartbroken for him. I had no idea he was carrying so much guilt in his heart. I let him cry it out for several minutes before speaking.

"Ramon, it's not your fault. You were just a kid. That responsibility shouldn't have been put on your shoulders. You were grieving your mother, and you had to take care of your father without any guidance. I'm not saying it's his fault, but it isn't yours either. You did what you could with what you were given."

I pull back, so that I can look into his eyes. "You need to let go of that guilt, Ramon. You're a good person, a good son, and a good friend."

He reaches in for another hug. "Thank you for saying that, Genny. Thank you so much."

Chapter 43

The next morning, I wake up around 6:00 a.m., and I notice that Ramon isn't in the room. I get up to go to the bathroom and brush my teeth. On my way back to the bed, I notice a sticky note on the coffee table.

> *Going to get some breakfast.*
> *I hope the kids like pancakes.*
> *-R*

I smile. I'm lucky to have a friend like Ramon in my life. He's an absolute sweetheart. I hope he knows how much I love him.

All three kids are still asleep, so I take the opportunity to shower. I'm worried about what's going to happen in the next few days. I don't even know where to start. Should I try speaking to Wallace in a civil way? Should I kick him out of our home? I don't even know my rights when it comes to these things. He co-owns everything we have. Maybe Ramon will know how to help.

I take a moment to let the events of the last month sink in. I haven't had much time to myself since Wallace came home from the hospital. When I think of him, all I want to do is cry. I've barely had the chance to grieve the husband I used to know and love. Yes, he was struggling with a lot of issues, but he was much more than that. He was amazing in so many ways. Who he was as a person made it worth the sacrifice of living with someone who suffered from such darkness. He made an effort to help himself get better. He made the effort for our marriage and our children. The man he's become since he's gotten sick shows no signs of the qualities he used to possess. For the past month, I've been holding on to the hope that the old Wallace is still in there somewhere, but now I need to accept that he's gone forever.

I think about Greg and some of the last things he said before falling to his death. He referred to his brain, or mental illness, as a disease and said there was no way of escaping it. After all these years, I'm finally starting to believe he might have been right. All the efforts, the progress, and the healing that Wallace went through, just to end up stepping a thousand feet backwards. His "disease," as Greg put it, has taken over, and there's no stopping it. It has invaded the Wallace I knew, the Wallace who wanted to fight. I'm afraid he has lost the battle, just like his brother and father.

As I'm finishing up in the bathroom, I hear Ramon return, accompanied by the aroma of pancakes and other breakfast food. I emerge from the bathroom wearing the same clothes as yesterday and my hair wrapped in a towel. Ramon smiles at me as he places the food on the coffee table.

"Cute," he teases.

Alaina is sitting on the sofa, reading a book from school. Lance and Maya are still sound asleep.

"How did you sleep, honey?" I ask Alaina.

"Not good," she says. "I kept having nightmares about Daddy hurting us."

My heart drops into my stomach. I wrap my arms around her small body and lift her chin, so I can see her beautiful dark brown eyes. I tuck a strand of hair behind her ear. I can see that she's hurting and scared.

"I'm sorry this is happening, sweetie. You know I'll do anything to protect the three of you, right?"

She nods.

"We're going to go back home as soon as possible. Daddy might not be there, but I'm not sure yet. Regardless, you and your siblings will be safe. Daddy won't hurt any of you."

"But what about you?" she asks. "What if he hurts you?"

"Don't worry about me, darling. Everything will be okay. I promise."

I fill a paper plate with her favourite breakfast foods, including a chocolate-chip pancake, a croissant, and some strawberries. She manages a tiny smile. "Thank you for bringing us breakfast, Ramon," she says.

"It's my pleasure, Alaina," Ramon replies.

I smile at their small encounter.

"So, what's the plan for today?" Ramon asks as I bite into a strawberry.

"I don't know what to do," I reply, feeling defeated. "I have to go back to the house eventually."

"I'll go with you and the kids. Maybe we can ask Daniel and Norman to come too to ensure that Wallace can't get to you or your children."

I nod in approval.

"You need to tell the police that he's threatened you. Then you need to get a restraining order against him and to start filing for a divorce. I have a friend who's been a lawyer for ten years. I can call him to see if he can help."

"Thank you so much, Ramon."

"No need to thank me," he replies, smiling.

Hearing all the steps I'm about to take to leave Wallace makes it all seem too real. Part of me wishes I could just wake up from this nightmare and go back to Wallace and the beautiful life we built together. It's surreal how everything can change so drastically in a matter of a few months.

I can't believe that the person I used to love more than anything is now the person I never want to see again.

Chapter 44

I'm back at the house accompanied by Ramon, Norman, and Daniel. My children were supposed to be here with us too, but after seeing the state that Wallace left the house in, I decided to drop them off at Robin's.

The house has been torn apart. Chairs are thrown across the living room, windows are broken, the cabinets are empty, and food and broken dishes are scattered everywhere. When I get to our bedroom, I find pink lipstick smeared all over our white duvet and on the carpet. Using the same lipstick, he has written "fucking whore" over and over again on the wall above our bed. Although the damage is repairable, he has forever tainted our home with this horrible memory. I feel sick to my stomach, seeing what he's capable of.

It takes two hours for all four of us to clean up everything that Wallace has destroyed. We also take photos of the damage to include in the police report that I plan to file later.

Earlier this morning, Robin and Daniel confirmed that Wallace didn't go by their homes last night. Mike and Vic haven't heard from him either. I'm relieved that he hasn't tried to terrorize our family and friends in the hopes of getting to me. Meanwhile, Ramon contacted his lawyer friend, Aaron, to see how long it will take to get a restraining order against Wallace.

"He said it could take up to a month to obtain a restraining order," Ramon tells me afterward, "but he might be able to pull some strings and get it done in a matter of days, especially if it's filed as an emergency. The only thing that might be difficult to do is to prove that he's been stalking and harassing you. This is why it's important for you to file a police report as soon as possible. Also, if he tries calling you again, we need to record him. However, the images showing how he destroyed your home should be sufficient proof that he's dangerous and a threat to you and your children. You'll also have all of us as witnesses of him harassing you."

"I can't believe this is Wallace we're talking about." Norman says. "He's always been the kindest, most caring guy I've ever met. I knew he had issues with his mental health in his past, but he's the last person I would have guessed to be capable of something so horrible." He shakes his head.

"I know," I reply, lowering my head. "I never thought that Wallace would become a man that I am afraid of.

Daniel puts his hand on my shoulder. "I'm so sorry that you're going through this, Gen. This is an absolute nightmare. I'm praying this will all be over soon. In the meantime, you have many people to love and support you through all of this."

"Thank you, Dan. I love you." I give him a hug.

"What's she doing here?" Ramon says.

I look out of the living room window and see Candace approaching the front door.

"I'll go see what she wants," Daniel says.

"No. I'm assuming she wants to speak to me," I say, anger burning inside. "I need to know how she found the audacity to show up here."

I open the front door and step outside before Candace makes it to the porch. I look back at the boys. "Please keep an eye on me through the window. I'll give you a signal if I need help." All three of them nod, then I close the door behind me and face Candace.

"How dare you come to my home after helping him do this to us!" I yell.

For the first time since meeting her, I see a glimpse of emotion in her expression.

"You don't understand, Genevieve. That's not at all what happened."

I just stare at her.

"Wallace reached out to me several days ago," she continues. "It was the first I had heard of him in over five years."

"I called you and Rhea as soon as he ended up in the hospital!" I reply. "You never bothered to call back. He almost died, and neither of you even cared."

"I changed my home phone number, and Rhea died a few months after Greg," she reveals, sounding way too casual.

My eyes widen. "What?"

"She died of a brain aneurysm in her sleep. It wasn't announced in the papers because I couldn't allow them to print it. It felt too hypocritical, since I knew that no one was going to miss her. There was no funeral. I got her cremated and then spread her ashes beside our father's grave. I gave almost everything in her apartment to Goodwill, and I threw the rest out."

My heart sinks. I was never close with Rhea, and she was never the most loving mother, but she was still my mother-in-law and I still felt an attachment to her. I thought that she was simply misunderstood, just like Greg and Wallace. I can't help but feel that Candace handled her death in a cruel way. She was still her mother, after all.

"How could you not tell Wallace?" I ask.

"He said he never wanted to see us again. I figured he wouldn't care."

"Yes, but did he really mean it?"

"He wouldn't have said it if he didn't mean it," she replies, her voice cold.

"So, why did you agree to see him when he called you?" I ask.

"He told me he got sick and almost died. He was hysterical on the phone. Crying, slurring his words, not making much sense. But then he told me that he thought that you had become evil and that you were plotting something against him. It reminded me of how Greg acted near the end. So, I decided to go pick him up that night.

When I saw his face, I knew something was wrong. He looked different in a way I couldn't explain."

"So, what happened?"

"He asked if he could live with me because you and the kids drove him crazy. He kept saying that you had all changed and that you'd been teaching the kids to hate him while he was in the hospital. He stayed at my house for three days, and it was hell. He would leave randomly in the middle of the night, and he would lose his temper with me over the smallest things. I kicked him out of my house because I was tired of dealing with his shit." It's funny how her experience is almost the same as mine.

"So, how did you end up following me to the café yesterday?"

"Yesterday morning, he called me over fifteen times at around ten o'clock. When I finally answered, he begged me to come get him because he suspected you were cheating on him. He told me that you were supposed to be at the psychiatrist's office for an appointment, and he wanted to make sure you were actually there. I know I shouldn't have fed into his delusions, but part of me was curious to know if his suspicions were correct. So, I picked him up, and we drove to Dr. Evians' office. He told me that your appointment was supposed to be until eleven, but we saw you storm out of there as soon as we arrived, and it was only a quarter past ten. That's when he begged me to follow you, and we did, which lead us to your father's house. We saw you getting into a car with that man, and we followed you, then saw you going into that coffee shop. Watching him observe you with that man made my skin crawl. He was completely livid, swearing and screaming at you from the car. It was madness. When he noticed you and the man staring in our direction, I drove off because I was afraid that he was going to get out of the car and cause a scene. I decided to drive him back home."

"The entire way back, I was trying to get him to calm down. I did everything I could to convince him that there was a reasonable explanation as to why you were out with another man, but he wasn't having it. He rushed inside the house, and went on a complete rampage. I was screaming at him to stop when he was tearing your house apart. He had suddenly stopped in his tracks, and started accusing me of choosing you over him. He started coming toward me, and he pushed me to the ground." She pauses.

Her face turns white as though she's reliving it.

She unzips her jacket to reveal huge purple bruises in the shape of fingers around her neck. My jaw drops.

"He almost killed me. While I was gasping for air, he told me I deserved to die because I was heartless like our mother. The only reason he didn't kill me was because he thought he heard you pull into the driveway. That's when he let me go and ran out the front door, which is when I made my escape. I haven't seen him since then. I have no idea where he ran off to," she says.

Her revelation of what happened makes me absolutely terrified of my husband. My heart drops to my stomach.

"Why didn't you call the police? Get him arrested?" I ask her this, not only wondering why she didn't do it to keep herself safe, but also to understand why she would risk for me and my children to also be in danger, by him still being out there.

"I didn't call the police because I owed it to him for what I had done the night he tried killing himself. I'm the one who orchestrated his attempt, and I never faced any consequences for it. I figured that he deserved that same chance," she says.

"Also," she continues, "I didn't do anything about it because I knew that he was right. I'm heartless like our mother. I wish I could say that I wasn't, but I can't continue to pretend that I'm not." She admits.

I shake my head in disbelief. "You don't really mean that," I tell her.

"Believe what you want. I'm not going to pretend that I care. This life has been so unfair to me, there's nothing keeping me from admitting it anymore," she says, bluntly.

"Regardless of the truth, what Wallace did to you is not okay. Aren't you afraid of who he's become?" I say, still trying to process everything she just revealed to me.

A smirk creeps to her face, making me feel uneasy.

"I've tried telling you this over fourteen years ago, Genevieve. Greg tried reminding you of it just before he died. Hell, he even tried to take care of it for you." She grins, appearing satisfied.

"What do you mean?" I ask.

"I expected him to turn out this way. It's the burden of the *disease*, Genevieve." She laughs. "He'll never escape it. Even after you thought you cured him, it found its way back, and it came with a *vengeance*." She shakes her head. "You should have listened. Instead, you chose to accept the burden of loving a broken mind. Now you and your children will have to pay the consequences." She has a sinister look in her eyes.

As her words echo inside my head, I want to scream. A tear runs down my cheek. “It’s not fair. It’s not his fault. Wallace doesn’t deserve this. He was such a kind soul.”

She shrugs in response, but her expression softens. She leans closer to me. “Good luck,” she whispers. “It’ll all be over soon.” She stares into my eyes before turning around and leaving.

I’m unable to speak as I attempt to digest our conversation. My head is spinning, and I feel light headed. I sit on the front porch and wrap my arms around my knees, trying to gather my thoughts.

I hear the front door open, and I turn to look at Ramon, who sits down next to me.

“What did she want?” he asks.

“I don’t even know where to begin,” I tell him, then I bury my face into my knees.

Chapter 45

It's been four days since Wallace trashed the house. The kids and I have been staying with Ramon, but we have decided to go back to the house today. Alaina and Lance want to return to school, and I agreed because I feel they'll be safer there. I inform the staff of what happened to ensure they remain vigilant in case Wallace shows up at the school.

Ramon's friend, Aaron, was able to get a judge to issue an emergency restraining order for me and the children after we submitted our testimonies and the photos of what Wallace did to our home. I tried to convince Candace to submit a photo of her neck and to provide a statement to the police, but she refused. Regardless, the evidence that we submitted was enough. However, they haven't been able to locate Wallace to serve him with the papers.

It's just past noon, and Ramon and I have packed the kids' bags and mine to head back home. We order some food to eat when we get there. Robin, her daughters, and my dad will join us in about twenty minutes. Robin decided to keep Nora home from school today.

We changed the locks of the front and back doors of the house to ensure that Wallace can't come in. Technically, he has a right to stay in his own home, but I would rather he bring me to court than give him access to the house.

When we arrive, there's no sign of a break-in, and everything in the house appears untouched. It looks like Wallace hasn't been in here since we left.

Despite how ridiculous that sounds, I still worry about his well-being. I can't imagine where he's staying right now. I called Justin a few nights ago to ask if Wallace is staying at his place, but he had no idea what I was talking about. Wallace doesn't have anyone else that he can turn to right now, so I don't know where he could be. It's as if he's vanished. These last few days have been agonizing. Every time I turn a corner, I expect him to show up. I feel like something horrible is bound to happen soon, and I'm terrified for my kids. All I want is for them to be safe.

It's been so difficult for me to explain to them what's going on. Alaina is older, so I've been a bit more truthful with her. However, Lance is only five, and he still looks up to his father and sees him as the greatest man in the world, just like Wallace used to be. Lance was afraid of him at times after he came home from the hospital, especially when he lashed out. Still, he would forget about it soon after, and it didn't make him see his father in a different light. He's too young to understand the severity of the situation, so he's been upset with me because he thinks I'm the reason that Wallace is gone. It hurts my heart that my son is angry with me, but I try to remind myself that I'm protecting his well-being.

Maya is even younger, so she doesn't really understand what's going on. I've noticed that she hasn't shown any signs of being upset that her father is gone. If anything, she's been more relaxed and energetic. I'm sure it's a relief for her not to see her father screaming and throwing objects at us anymore.

As a mother, I try my best to shield my kids from what's going on around them, but it's been almost impossible to do that. When Wallace started acting violent, I wanted to stay and work through it with him for the sake of our family. I realize now that holding on for as long as I did likely did more harm than good.

I set our bags on the couch in the living room as Ramon put the food on the kitchen counter.

"Mommy, can I go play in my room?" Maya asks.

"Yes, sweetheart. But let me go check up there first," I say. I walk upstairs to her bedroom and look inside. I also look in the closet and under her bed, but there's nothing out of the ordinary.

"Okay. I'll tell you when to come to the table for lunch," I say on my way out of the room. "Please keep the door open, so I can hear you. Grandpa, Auntie Robin, and your cousins are coming over soon."

"Okay, Mommy!" she replies.

I head back to the living room and unpack the bags with our dirty clothes from the hotel, then head for the basement stairs, my arms piled high with clothes, on my way to the laundry room.

Ramon laughs. "Do you have a laundry basket for those?"

"Yes, downstairs," I reply, feeling sheepish. "I thought there was a lot less stuff. Otherwise, I would've waited until I got downstairs to remove it all from the bags."

He chuckles. "Wait there one second." Ramon runs downstairs and comes back up with a laundry basket. Once I dump the clothes into it, he takes it back down to the laundry room for me.

"Thank you," I say when he comes back up.

He smirks. "You're welcome, Genny."

While waiting for everyone else to arrive, Ramon helps me set the table.

"After lunch, I have a few guys who are going to stop by to help me install a home security system for you," he says as he places the plates on the table. Ramon only felt comfortable allowing me to return home if I let him install a security system with cameras around the house. He was worried that Wallace would be able to enter easily otherwise.

"Unfortunately, it won't be the best because it's not *my* company's security system." He winks. "But it should do just fine. The guys that are coming are good friends of mine who I met through this business, and they owe me a favour."

"Sounds good. Thank you," I reply, with a smile.

About five minutes later, someone knocks at the door. For a moment, my heart sinks, but then I realize it's just Robin and my dad. I take a deep breath.

"You okay?" Ramon asks.

"Yes, sorry. I'm fine."

Ramon opens the door to greet everyone.

"Ramon, it's so nice to see you!" Robin gives him a hug.

"I know. I wish it was under different circumstances." He forces a laugh.

She gives a sympathetic look. "I know. We appreciate how much you've done for Gen in the last several days. Also, I'm sorry about the passing of your father. My sincerest condolences." She puts one hand on her heart and her other hand on his shoulder. He places his hand on top of hers.

"Thank you so much, Robin. It means a lot."

My dad gives me a big hug. "I'm so sorry, baby. I've been thinking of you nonstop." He places his hands on my cheeks, his eyes glistening with tears. "It kills me that I can't protect you and the kids as much as I want to." A tear falls to his cheek. The grief of my mom's passing has aged him. He's become a lot frailer in recent years. It's heartbreaking to see him unable to do all the things that he used to. It's an instant reminder of how fragile life is and how quickly youth can fade.

"I know, Daddy. You're still beyond capable of protecting me. Thank you for helping me through this." I wipe his tears with my thumb and kiss him on the cheek.

Maya runs down the stairs to greet everyone. She hugs Nora and Chloe first. As I watch them interact, I admire their innocence. I wish I could freeze time and cherish such moments for longer.

"Okay, girls, we're going to set you up at the children's table in the living room," I say. "Go take your seats. I'll have a plate out for you in a minute."

Maya and Nora each hold one of Chloe's hands as they walk over to the table together. I love the way that Nora and Maya interact with Chloe. They take care of her as if she's their child. It's the sweetest thing.

I take out three paper plates and place a serving of food in each one. Ramon and I picked up Chinese food for lunch. Robin takes the food to the girls.

"I'll help Chloe eat, Mommy," Nora says.

"Okay, hon." Robin replies.

Robin and I walk back to the dining table, where Ramon and my dad are already serving themselves.

"So, Wallace hasn't shown up since the restraining order has been issued?" Robin asks before shoving a spoonful of rice into her mouth.

"No. I have no idea where he is," I reply. "I'm still worried that he might show up at one of your houses."

My father has been staying with Robin for the last few days. Since he's elderly and living alone, we've been too afraid that Wallace might show up at his house, and he wouldn't be able to defend himself.

"Dad, you can come stay with me until they find him," I say. "Ramon is installing a security system with cameras. You'll be safer here than at home. Besides, I think it would be better for me not to stay alone here with the kids."

"Well, you wouldn't be entirely alone, I don't think." My dad smirks and turns to Ramon, whose face turns a light shade of pink.

"Uh, I think what Bob means is I'm going to stay in town longer than I had planned," Ramon says.

"But I can still stay over, sweetheart," my dad says, trying not to embarrass Ramon further. "I'd be delighted to."

"You're staying in town for how much longer?" I ask, trying not to sound too hopeful. I'm glad Ramon is staying but not for the reason my dad is implying. I just feel so much safer having another man around.

"A month, I think. Afterwards, I'll have no choice but to go back. The company will fall apart if I stay away too long," he says, grinning.

"Oh, I'm sure it's already fallen apart!" Robin adds, and we all laugh.

It feels nice to have a meal together and a light-hearted conversation for once. It's been months since I've been able to escape the nightmare I've been living through. It's good to think of something other than how much I'm hurting.

Unfortunately, I know it's going to be short-lived.

After lunch, Robin helps the girls wash up in the bathroom while my Dad helps me clean up the table. Ramon is rinsing the dishes. I look at the time and realize it's already 2:45 p.m. I have to pick up Alaina and Lance from school in about fifteen minutes.

Suddenly, I hear my cell phone ring. I reach for it on the counter, where it's been charging, and bring it to my ear.

"Hello?" Several seconds go by, and no one speaks on the other end of the line, but I can hear someone breathing. Everyone else stops in their tracks, waiting and listening.

"Hello? Who is this? I can hear you," I say, sounding impatient. Fear grows inside of me, and I hear my heart pounding as I hold the phone against my ear.

"Genevieve," a voice whispers. "You need to come now." Just as I'm trying to figure out who it is, a bomb drops. "He has a gun. I think he saw me talking with you outside the other day. I think he wants to kill me. You need to get here now."

It's Candace. My heart rate shoots up.

"I'll call the police. They'll come to you."

"They won't get here fast enough! He's been yelling your name over and over. He's going to kill me before they get here. Please, I beg you," she sobs. "He has Lance."

Her last three words make my knees go weak.

"He has Lance!" I cry, running toward the door. "She told me he has a gun, and he has Lance!"

Ramon is right behind me. He grabs my arm. "You can't go there, Gen! It's too dangerous! You could get killed!"

"He has my baby! I need to save him! I can't let him do this!" I'm hysterical now.

"I'll call 911," Robin says, hurrying down the stairs with the girls. "Was that Candace?"

"Yes!" I reply, barely able to think clearly. I grab my keys and run out the door.

"I'll drive, Gen!" Ramon says, taking my keys from me.

"Someone call Daniel, and tell him to pick up Alaina from school!" Ramon yells.

Chapter 46

We arrive at Candace's house in under a minute. I run to the front door. Ramon pushes in front of me, stopping me from going inside.

"Gen, think about this. I know Lance is in there, but you can't risk leaving your children without a mother. Let me go first."

"Okay," I reply, nodding.

I stand behind Ramon, who is carrying a baseball bat. He told me on the way here that he also has a pocket knife in his jacket. He turns the doorknob with his free hand and pushes the door open.

Once inside, we find Candace backed up in the corner of the living room with Wallace pointing a shotgun at her. Ramon and I freeze. When Wallace sees us, he throws his head back and laughs. His expression is dark, and his eyes are filled with agony. He appears to be suffering from what he's become, and it's horrifying to watch.

My eyes dart between Candace and Wallace. "Where the fuck is Lance?" I demand.

Wallace frowns. "Lance?" he appears to have no idea what I'm talking about. I realize Candace lied about Lance being there to ensure I came. She set me up!

"You backstabbing bitch," I mumble, though it's loud enough for the others to hear. "I should've known."

"Oh, so you told them Lance was here?" Wallace asks. "That's why they showed up?" He laughs again, even harder. I stay behind Ramon, terrified of what Wallace is about to do. As he laughs, the shotgun shakes. Then he stops laughing, and an angry look fills his face as he stares at Ramon and me.

"You shouldn't have done that, Genevieve. I was getting better. You fucked it all up!" He shakes his head as he approaches us.

"Done what, Wallace?"

"Him." An evil grin appears on his face as he points to Ramon.

"I didn't cheat on you! You know Ramon is just a friend!" My voice shakes with fear as he comes within inches of my face.

"I'm not *just* worried about your cheating, Genevieve!" he screams. "Even though, I have to admit, it doesn't surprise me. I knew that you two looked too close on our wedding night." He turns to face Ramon. "I don't blame you. She's a real *Gem*." He smirks, and Ramon flinches under Wallace's gaze.

"Why are you doing this?" I ask, tears streaming down my face. "It doesn't have to come to this, Wallace! You can still get help. If you leave without hurting anyone, you can still get better. You can be free! Don't listen to Candace or Greg. You don't have to let the darkness win. You can continue to fight. You can fight for me and for our children! You can still overcome this. Prove them wrong!"

"Prove them wrong or prove you right?" he asks. His blank stare makes my skin crawl.

"What do you mean?" I reply.

"You always saw me as a project, Genevieve. Someone to fix. Well, guess what? You can't fix me, Gen! How many times do we have to tell you that? You couldn't accept me as I was. You wanted to bury a part of me that makes me who I am! As soon as that part of me became stronger, you abandoned me! I saw the way you looked at me when I woke up in the hospital. You had already given up on me. I saw it in your eyes!" Tears fall down his face and drip down his neck. His eyes are red and irritated. "You've tried to repress the real me for all these years, and now look at what you've done!"

The way his mind twists things is almost fascinating. It shatters my heart to know this is what he thinks of me, as if the last eighteen years never happened.

"Stop lying, Wallace. This isn't the real you. The real you would never do something like this."

"You have no idea how tormenting it was to pretend for all these years," he replies. "To suppress these urges to be my true self. Somehow you convinced me that the boring life that we led was what happiness looks like! Now I realize that was all bullshit."

His words pierce my heart like a knife. I fall to my knees, crying. Ramon crouches next to me.

I lift my head up and notice Candace looking around the room as if she's trying to figure out how to escape. Her eyes lock with mine, and I nod in her direction to show that I'm aware of what she's thinking. Ramon notices our exchange.

"What do you want me to do about it, Wallace?" I ask.

"You can set me free. You can disappear!"

He charges at me, and Ramon swings the baseball bat. He hits Wallace on the shoulder, causing him to drop the shotgun, which clatters across the room.

Candace is still in the corner. She can't reach for the gun because Wallace is in the way.

Wallace wrenches the baseball bat away from Ramon and then punches him in the face, causing him to fall to the floor. He gets on top of him and starts hitting him, repeatedly. Blood splatters with every blow.

I reach for his arm and scream at him to stop, but he elbows me in the nose, sending me stumbling back.

Wallace gets off Ramon, who is now unconscious, and grabs me by the collar. He smashes the back of my head against the front door, then pins me against it. I feel a sharp pain at the back of my head and blood dripping from my hair. He hit my head onto one of the door hinges, which slashed my scalp.

Out of the corner of my eye, I notice Candace has left the room, and she took the shotgun with her. I assume she's made a run for it.

Ramon's body looks lifeless. Tears stream down my face as I stare at it.

Wallace grabs my neck with both hands and pushes against my windpipe. "It'll all be over soon, my sweet little

Gem." His sinister eyes stare into mine as he reiterates the same words Candace told me a few days prior. I struggle to breathe, trying to free his hands from my throat.

"Wallace, please..."

He squeezes harder, causing me to gasp for air. I feel a sharp pain in my throat as his hands crush my trachea. I try to scream, but nothing comes out.

I shut my eyes, knowing it is most likely my last few moments of life. I think of my babies and how I've failed them. I brought them into this world, and now I'm leaving them, orphaned.

As I lose consciousness, a loud sound makes my ears pop. Then everything goes dark.

Chapter 47

I wake up to blinding lights. I squint as I try to adjust. As monitors beep around me, I try to focus on my surroundings. I notice an IV in my arm and feel a tube up my nose.

"Baby girl?" my dad says. My vision is blurry, but I can make out his silhouette beside my bed. "She's awake!" he exclaims.

"Dad?" I try to speak, but a sharp pain shoots down my throat. I start to panic. He takes my hand in his.

"It's okay, baby. You're in the hospital. You hit your head pretty hard, and you lost consciousness due to a lack of oxygen. Your throat hurts because you suffered a tracheal rupture. Do you remember what happened?"

My eyes widen as it all comes rushing back to me. Wallace hitting my head against the door. His hands encircling my throat as he tries strangling me. Hearing the sound of my windpipe crushing beneath his grip. I raise my hand to my throat and feel the swollen bruises his fingers burnt into my neck. I feel nauseous, like I'm going to throw up.

My dad notices me heaving and brings a cup to my mouth, allowing me to expel the contents of my stomach, along with blood. I wince in pain, then grab my throat to ease the throbbing. I start to sob.

"It's okay, baby." Dad rubs my back as I continue crying, feeling helpless.

Dr. Embrun enters the room with a nurse. "Oh, Genevieve," he says as he approaches the foot of my bed, wincing at the blood dripping from my chin.

"Don't worry," the nurse says. "We'll get you cleaned up." She takes the cup from my dad and then wipes my mouth with a wet cloth.

"I'm glad to see you're awake, Genevieve," Dr. Embrun says. "You had surgery to fix a fracture in your windpipe. It's normal to expel blood from the throat after a tracheal injury. You might cough up blood every now and then while you're recovering. If you expel a substantial amount of blood after you're discharged, come back to the hospital immediately. We wouldn't want you to hemorrhage."

I try to speak again. "Wallace" is all I manage to get out.

"Your husband is currently in the ICU. The police arrived at the scene as he was strangling you. Wallace was shot near the chest, and the trauma from the gunshot wound caused him to have an ischemic stroke. That means a blockage hindered blood flow to his brain. The doctors were able to remove the blockage, but there's a high probability that the damage is irreversible. He's in a coma, and we're still assessing the brain damage he incurred as a result of the stroke. With his history of severe brain trauma from just a few months ago, his chances of recovery or even survival are relatively low." He lowers his head. "If he does survive, he'll be charged with attempted murder and transported to the nearest correctional facility to continue his treatment until his court date.

I'm relieved to hear those words.

It feels surreal that just a few months ago, the thought of Wallace dying was my worst fear. Now I'm more worried about him surviving. I'm definitely not praying for his recovery this time around.

"My babies?" I ask.

"They're with Robin and Norman," my dad assures me. "They'll come by once you feel a bit better."

"Yes, you need to allow your throat to rest and recover for a few days," Dr. Embrun says. "Try not to talk for the next few hours. Otherwise, you might strain your vocal cords, which will be painful. You should be able to start speaking a bit more by tomorrow morning."

"Well, that's definitely going to be hard for her," my dad quips. I manage a smile. I love that he can still bring some humour to such a traumatic experience.

Dr. Embrun looks into my eyes with his pen light, checks the swelling of the lymph nodes in my neck, and listens to my heart and lungs.

"Everything looks good," he says. "Luckily, there's no sign of severe damage to your brain from when you hit the back of your head on the door hinge. You did suffer a mild concussion, but the headaches and light sensitivity should subside in a few weeks. They had to stitch up the wound at the back of your scalp, but the stitches should be ready to come out within a week. I'm thankful that all of your injuries were treatable, Genevieve. I'm so sorry this happened to you." Dr. Embrun gives me a sympathetic look and places a hand on my shoulder. My eyes start to water again.

"I know she wants to thank you, so I'll say it for her," Dad says. "Thank you for taking care of my baby girl, Dr. Embrun. You have no idea how grateful we are." My dad's voice cracks as his eyes fill with tears.

"Genevieve is a strong gal," Dr. Embrun says. "She pulled through all on her own." He steps back from my bed. "Okay, get some rest, Genevieve. I'll come and check on you in a few hours."

"I'm so happy you're okay," my dad says once Dr. Embrun and the nurse leave my room. "I love you so much, baby." He kisses my hand. I place my other hand on his cheek. He places his forehead against mine and cries while holding my fist in his hands, kissing it repeatedly. "I don't know what I would've done if I had lost you."

I rub his cheek with my thumb as his tears fall onto my face.

Eventually, he lets go and sits in his chair. He spots a notepad and pen on the table next to my bed. He passes it to me. "Here, sweetheart. You can use this to write instead of talking. In case there's anything you want to say."

I scribble a short note.

Where's Ramon?

"Ramon is okay. He was admitted into the ICU at the same time as you. He had to have an emergency surgery to decompress the rapid swelling of his brain, which was caused by Wallace hitting him repeatedly."

My heart stops. Oh, Ramon. I want to scream at the thought of him suffering a brain injury because of Wallace.

"Luckily, they were able to relieve the pressure as soon as he arrived at the hospital, and he's expected to make a full recovery. It's the middle of the night, so he's likely sleeping right now, but I'm sure he'll be able to come visit in the morning." I sigh in relief. Then I write another question on the notepad.

Where's Candace?

"She hasn't been seen since that night. She was declared a missing person around three days ago."

I'm stunned by the news. Where has Candace gone with the shotgun?

"There's an ongoing search for her. She's a suspect in the events that transpired that night. They think she might've been an accomplice in Wallace's attempt to kill you. The police have already obtained phone records from the conversation you had with her before you showed up at her house. They know she lied about Wallace having Lance with him at her house in order to trick you."

I'm not sure if Candace helped Wallace plan his attempt to murder me. She's troubled, and she's far from trustworthy, but I don't believe she tried to kill me. She was just trying to survive, like she's been doing her entire life. I feel crazy for defending her, but I'm trying to put myself in her shoes as someone who lacks empathy and suffers from so much unresolved trauma. She admitted to me that she was done caring about how she was perceived by others. Her revelation shows that all the times she helped me were merely attempts to help her own image. Once that was no longer a priority for her, she didn't care what happened to me.

I write one last question for my father to answer.

How long have I been in the hospital?

He looks at me. "Eight days, sweetheart."

...

My dad stays with me until I fall asleep. When I wake up the next morning, I have a pounding headache, and my throat is on fire. It's 7:00 a.m., and a nurse just brought my breakfast. They took out my feeding tube about an hour ago, and they're only going to serve me soft foods for the duration of my stay. My meal consists of Jell-O, watered-down oatmeal, and bone broth. None of it looks appetizing, but I'm starving.

I swallow a spoonful of bone broth, which soothes my aching throat. I notice how hard it is to lift my arm and feed myself. It's frustrating how weak I've gotten since being in the hospital. I look up at the nurse, who is changing out my saline IV bag.

"Can I go for a walk to see a friend who's staying on this floor?" I ask. My throat still hurts when I talk, but it's a huge improvement from last night.

"Of course, dear. I'll come back and get you as soon as you finish your breakfast." She gives me a warm smile.

After I manage to eat half of my breakfast, the nurse returns. She unhooks my IV but keeps the port in my arm. She has a wheelchair with her that I can use in case I feel too weak to stand.

She helps me out of bed and then gives me a moment to get my balance. It feels weird standing after being in bed for over a week. I manage to walk into the hallway, but my steps are painfully slow. I'm desperate to see Ramon to make sure he's okay.

His room is just on the other end of the hallway, but it's quite a struggle to get there. Once inside his door, I sink into the wheelchair, and the nurse wheels me up to his bed. Ramon turns toward me, and I'm shocked when I see his face.

It's covered with purple and yellow bruises, and he has about ten stitches near his eyebrow. His head is shaved, and he has staples in his scalp from his surgery. Tears fill my eyes at the sight of it.

"Oh my God, Ramon. I'm so sorry. This is all my fault." I bury my face in my hands, ashamed that he had suffered all of this because of me.

"Hey, Genny, no. It's okay. I know it looks bad, but I promise you, I'm fine. Please don't cry. I'll be okay." He leans toward me and takes me into his arms, rubbing my back in an effort to comfort me.

"I'm so sorry Wallace did this to you. I should have begged you not to follow me."

"You know I wouldn't have listened, Genny. I couldn't risk you going alone. I should have stopped you."

"You knew I wouldn't have been able to live with myself if something happened to Lance," I say. "We both thought he was there with Wallace." I cringe at the thought of everything that happened that night.

"You're right," Ramon says. "Regardless, what matters is that we both made it out alive. I was so worried about you."

I look into his kind eyes. "I was worried about you too. Before I lost consciousness, I thought you were dead. I'm so thankful you're alive and that you're going to make a full recovery. Have you heard about Wallace?"

"Yeah. Your dad told me what happened. I can't believe he survived a gunshot wound to the chest."

"I know," I reply, nodding. "Is it bad that I feel kind of sad that he's going to die?"

He gives me a sympathetic look. "Oh, Genny. I don't know many people who would understand, but I do. He's your husband. You spent almost half your lifetime with him. Just a few months ago, he was the love of your life. Neither your heart nor your mind can forget that kind of love so quickly. You're going to grieve him for a long time. You haven't even grieved the part of him that you lost when he got sick. Please, don't feel ashamed for the feelings you have toward him. You're allowed to be sad, you're allowed to mourn, and you're allowed to miss the part of him that you fell in love with. It breaks my heart that he robbed you of all of the beautiful memories that you shared together. When you think of him, try to remember those moments instead of the ones that lead up to the end."

His words make me start crying again. I think I've cried enough in the last eighteen years for many lifetimes.

"I really needed to hear that, Ramon. Thank you." I put my hand in his. "Do you have room for one more?" I ask, pointing at his bed. "If not, I'll make room."

He scooches to one side of the bed. I grin as I climb in beside him. After a brief struggle, we make it work. I lay my head on his chest near his heart, soothed by the sound of his heartbeat. A few minutes later, I drift off to sleep.

Chapter 48

The nurse wakes me around twenty minutes later, telling me I need to head back to my room because I have visitors. She wheels me back, and I'm greeted by many familiar faces.

"Mommy!" Alaina, Lance, and Maya exclaim. They run to me, and I give all three of them a long, much-needed hug.

"My babies. I've missed you so much."

Alaina looks at me, and her eyes widen with concern.

"Mommy, what are those bruises on your neck?" she asks, her voice trembling.

"Those are from the accident, sweetheart," Robin says. "Mommy will be okay. Don't worry." Alaina seems to buy that explanation. Robin tells me later that she explained to the kids that Ramon, Wallace and I got into a car accident and that Wallace is in a coma now because of it.

"Is Daddy going to die?" Lance asks me.

"I don't know, sweetheart. We'll know more about what's going on with Daddy soon." I'm not ready to have the conversation with them if Wallace survives and ends up going to jail.

"Come on, guys. Give Mommy some space, so she can head back into her bed," Robin says.

As they move to the other side of the room, my dad helps me out of the wheelchair and guides me back into bed. It makes me smile to see him so eager to help.

"Thank you, Daddy," I say.

"Just count yourself lucky that your old man still has a bit of strength left in him." He laughs. When he places me down on the bed, he kisses me on the forehead.

Robin sits at the foot of my bed and takes my hand in hers. "I was worried sick, Gen. You have no idea the relief I felt when I got the call from Dad telling me that you woke up." Tears run down her cheeks. "I love you so much," she says.

"I love you too, Robin," I reply, smiling. "You know I could never leave you. And thanks so much for taking care of the kids."

"Anytime, sis. I can't take all the credit, though. Mike and Vic have helped out a lot as well. They took them for a few nights this week. They're coming by to see you in a few hours."

"It doesn't surprise me at all that they offered to help."

I take a moment to think about my amazing support system. Despite the tragedies I've endured, I've always had these extraordinary people by my side to help me. I don't think I could have survived without them.

"Any new news on Candace? Were they able to find her?" I ask.

"No. They still don't know where she is," Robin replies. "They haven't located the gun either, so there's a chance that she still has it."

Hearing that makes me nervous. I won't rest until she's found. I never thought she would want to hurt me, but then again, she's been deceitful, manipulative, and conniving ever since I've known her. I don't know what she's capable of. I hope she's found soon.

A young woman who looks like a doctor enters the room. "Mrs. Browne?" she asks, looking around. I cringe upon hearing the last name I have yet to change.

"Yes?"

"I'd like to talk to you about your husband. Is there somewhere we can speak in private?"

"I'll take the kids down for a snack at the cafeteria." Robin says. "We'll be right back." I nod as she leads them out of the room.

"I want my dad to stay, if that's okay," I tell her.

"Of course," she replies. "I'm Dr. Newton. I'm the attending physician who has taken on your husband's care since he arrived at the hospital. We have just completed our final neurological assessment with Dr. Hosh, and we have found no level of brain activity. I'm sorry, Mrs. Browne, but your husband is what we consider 'brain dead.'"

I'm speechless, unable to shed a tear. "Thanks for letting me know. When will you unplug him?" I ask.

She appears stunned from my bluntness. "Um, we were going to give you a few days to discuss options, but if you feel that you're ready, we can discuss them now."

"I don't need a few days," I reply. "Please give me the options." I just want this to end.

She names a few different options, all of which result in Wallace eventually being taken off life support.

"Since he's on a ventilator, we can simply turn it off and let him go naturally," she says. "It should happen peacefully. Also, I'd like to ask..." She consults his chart. "Wallace isn't registered as an organ donor. Would you consent to him donating his organs upon his passing?"

I know that such patients make the best organ donors. I also know that the Wallace I fell in love with would want this chance to save lives.

"Of course," I reply, managing a smile.

"Thank you for confirming. We will prepare your husband, so you and your family can say your final goodbyes. A nurse will come get you in about half an hour."

"Thank you, Dr. Newton," I reply. She nods and then leaves the room.

Soon after, Robin and the kids return. My heart sinks as I see my babies' smiling faces. They have no idea about the bad news I'm about to share with them.

I look at my dad, hoping to receive some advice.

"You can do this," he whispers. I nod and then turn back to my kids.

"Babies, come and sit with Mommy for a minute. I need to tell you something important."

Chapter 49

My heart breaks, seeing all three of my children crying for their father. I try to explain it to them in a way that they can understand, also making sure to emphasize how much their daddy loved them. As much as he was the cause of many traumas in our lives, I still want them to think of their father as a good person. They deserve to hold onto those memories from before he got sick. I don't want them to remember the tainted versions that I've been stuck with.

After about an hour, the nurse comes by to walk us to Wallace's room. On our way there, we stop by to see Ramon, so he can join us if he wants to. He follows us as we go to see Wallace's body, lying lifeless in the bed. He's attached to the ventilator, so I have to warn the kids that it might look a bit scary. They take it well when they see him.

"Can I go closer to him Mommy?" Maya asks.

"Of course, baby. You can all go closer to him. Just make sure not to touch anything."

Lance and Maya approach the bed, but Alaina stays behind.

"You don't want to go see him, sweetie?" I ask.

She shakes her head, her eyes brimming with tears. "I can't. I don't want this to be my last memory of him."

"I understand, hon. You don't have to."

"You know what, sweetheart?" my dad says. "We can go back to your mommy's room and wait for everyone there. What do you think of that?"

She nods, then takes his hand when he holds it out to her. "I'm sorry, Daddy," she says as she lowers her head. I can hear the pain in her voice. My poor baby. She has gone through way too much in her young life. I would do anything to take her pain away.

"Take your time. I'll take care of her," my dad whispers in my ear before leaving the room.

"Please don't go, Daddy." Maya lays her head on Wallace's abdomen and cries. "I don't want you to leave forever. I'm going to miss you."

Tears roll down my cheeks as I watch my two babies say goodbye to their father. I'm doing everything I can to keep it together for them. Ramon notices my reaction and takes my hand, squeezing it.

Lance takes Wallace's hand.

"Daddy, I didn't know I would never get to play dinosaurs with you again," Lance says. "If I would have known, I wouldn't have been bad. I'm sorry for making you angry sometimes. I hope you still think I'm a good boy."

Hearing Lance say that makes me fall apart. As much as I've tried to mask what was going on, they still managed to absorb so much. My heart breaks for what my poor babies have gone through. I try to wipe my tears as they come, but they're falling too quickly. Robin passes me a few tissues.

"Okay, we're ready for you to go up to heaven, Daddy. We love you," Lance says. Maya kisses his hand, then walks back toward us. Lance follows.

"Okay, I'm going to shut off the life support now," the nurse says. "Are you ready?" Dr. Newton is also in the room with us to witness the nurse disconnect the ventilator.

"Yes, we're ready," I reply. I hold my children's hands and walk toward Wallace's bed until we're by his side. The nurse unplugs the ventilator, and after a few moments, the heart monitor starts beeping, showing a flatline.

Suddenly, Wallace's eyes flicker open, sending a shock of fear up my body. I look into his eyes, expecting to see the same darkness that overcame him moments before he almost killed me. Instead, I see nothing. Total emptiness. I sigh in relief and hold on to Lance and Maya as they sob. I look at Ramon and Robin.

Thank God it's over.

Chapter 50

Thirteen days have gone by since Wallace passed away. I'm back home, and I'm continuing to recover from the injuries I sustained. My children are still mourning their father, but they are already starting to adjust to his absence. Wallace's funeral is later today. I've decided to have one for the sake of my children. Our family and friends will be in attendance. I've also decided to put the house up for sale, so my family and I can move on from everything that has happened.

An investigation was still taking place at Candace's house just before Wallace passed, since it was still part of the crime scene, and Candace had yet to be found. While searching her property, they found human remains buried under her shed. Apparently, the smell of a decomposing corpse can last for years in an enclosed area. The remains belonged to Rhea.

Soon after the discovery, Candace was found dead in a river near the bridge close to her house. She had used the shotgun on herself, dying instantly. I wish I could say I found what she did to Rhea shocking; however, the signs were all there after everything she had done to Wallace. I feel naïve for thinking she deserved a chance at redemption. Once her death was confirmed, I felt like I could take a breath for the first time in months. I suppose the darkness overcame her too. It was simply disguised differently.

Ramon was discharged from the hospital a few days after me. He is staying at my house, sleeping on the couch. He's heading back to Vancouver after the funeral, so we want to spend some time together before he left.

"Are you ready?" Ramon asks as he enters the living room, fiddling with his tie. He's wearing a black suit. I adjust his collar for him.

"Ready," I say with fake enthusiasm.

We head to the funeral home, picking up my father on the way. Everyone else is already there. When the doors open, the kids head toward their cousins, and I approach the small crowd of my loved ones.

"Thank you so much for coming," I say to Vic and Mike.

"We're so sorry for your loss, Gen," Vic replies as she hugs me.

"You're the strongest person we know, Gen." Mike says, hugging me as well.

Daniel and Linda come up to me soon after. "This is the beginning of a better life," Dan whispers in my ear.

I squeeze his shoulder. “I know, Danny. I’m looking forward to it.” I smile, then I look around at the venue and admire its beauty. All I can think of is my mother, since the last time we were there was for her funeral.

“I can’t imagine how Mom would have reacted to everything that happened,” I say. “As much as I’ve wished for her to be with me during the difficult times, I’m grateful she never had to witness such cruelty. It would have destroyed her.”

I thought this day was going to make me relive the trauma of the last few months, but it’s having the opposite effect. I feel nothing but peace, knowing this is the end of a horrible chapter in our lives. I feel sadness and grief for Wallace, but I’m learning how to cherish the love that I had with him over the last eighteen years. Some of the last things he said to me will haunt me for the rest of my life, but I know it wasn’t really him who said or did those awful things. I know the Wallace I loved, the Wallace I married, was kind, thoughtful, and warm. I hope that, eventually, I can forget the darkness that overcame him and remember how tragically beautiful our story was.

Ramon looks away from a conversation that he’s having with Robin and Norman when he notices me across the room. He leans over to say something in Robin’s ear, then walks over and gives me a hug.

“First you go to Vancouver straight after my wedding, and now you go back to Vancouver straight after my husband’s funeral. How dare you?” I say teasingly, which makes him laugh.

“I know, Gen. I wish I didn’t have to go back, but I have to finalize some things first.”

"What do you mean *finalize*? What do you have to finalize?"

"My buddy and I are moving our business to Toronto." A huge grin grows across his face. "I'm coming back home, where I belong." His eyes glow with joy.

"Oh my God, Ramon, you have no idea how happy that makes me!" I jump into his arms and hug him. Then I try to compose myself, remembering we're at my husband's funeral. "I'm so happy to have you back in my life, Ramon," I say, unable to hide my smile.

"So am I, Genny. I never should have left, knowing you were still here." A sultry look appears in his eyes when he locks his gaze with mine. My heart skips a beat.

"We should go take a seat. The service is starting soon," Robin says, bringing me back to earth.

"Um, yes. Of course." I feel my face grow warm. Robin has a suspicious grin on her face. She takes me by the arm and leads me away from Ramon.

"What was that?" she asks, giving me a suggestive look.

"I have no idea," I reply, feeling shy.

"I knew this was going to happen eventually," she says. "It's been brewing since high school! I just didn't expect it to happen at your husband's funeral."

"Shut up, Robin! It was nothing. I can't even think about that right now."

"Maybe not, but I *know* something awoke in you just now. And something has *definitely* awoken in him."

I don't answer because I know she's right.

...

When we arrive home after the funeral, I look through the boxes that Wallace kept in our closet to see if I can find anything of sentimental value for the kids. As I sift through piles of papers and photos, I notice a document labelled "insurance." I open the envelope, and I find an insurance policy that Wallace took out on March 20, 1996, the day after Greg died.

I read through the document, and notice a clause that catches my attention.

> In the event of the insured's death, the payee will disburse an amount of $1,000,000.00 to the beneficiary(ies) upon reception of the official death certificate of the insured. The beneficiary(ies) are entitled to the full disbursement considering they are not deceased within thirty days of the insured's death. Otherwise, the aforementioned disbursement will be made out to the insured's estate.
>
> Named beneficiary:
> Genevieve Browne. Spouse.

My jaw drops. How come Wallace never told me about this? Witnessing what happened to Greg that night must've really worried him. I'm in shock that he did this in secret. I'm feeling so many different emotions, it feels like my heart is going to burst. I picture Wallace getting this insurance policy, worrying about his family's well-being, and having no idea of what the future held. Unless maybe he did it because he could feel it coming. Perhaps he had an intuition that something bad was going to happen to him. Regardless of the reason, he did it, and it makes me feel close to him again for the first time in months.

Ramon walks past my room and notices me crying while surrounded by papers and photos scattered across the floor. He comes in and crouches next to me.

"What's wrong?" he asks.

"Read this." I pass the document to him. As Ramon reads it, his eyes widen.

"Oh my God, Genny," he says, scratching his head in disbelief.

"I know," I reply, crying.

Ramon picks up the envelope, and a piece of paper falls onto the pile on the floor. He picks it up, reads it, then smiles and hands it to me.

"What is it?" I ask.

"Just read it," he says.

I take the paper from him and recognize the handwriting on it right away.

Until your last breath, my Gem. Just like I promised.
I love you.
- Wallace

Tears blur my vision as I read those words over and over again. I press the small note to my heart and close my eyes. This is the sign of the old Wallace that I've been waiting for. The hope that I've been holding onto this entire time. This is the Wallace I know. This is the Wallace I will always love.

Epilogue

2014

The summer breeze blows through my hair while I sit outside by the pool. It's a beautiful, sunny Saturday. We're nearing the end of June, which means the kids and I are going to be on summer break soon. It's the best time of the year. I get to spend most of my time with the kids, and we get to do so many things together as a family. We've managed to heal over the last ten years, and I'm grateful for every day where I get to feel this good.

"Genny, do you want me to get you a drink?" Ramon asks through the patio door.

"Yes, please," I reply. Ramon comes running back with a strawberry daiquiri and hands it to me. "Thank you so much, babe," I tell him, then give him a quick kiss on the lips.

"Anything for my beautiful lady," he replies, grinning.

I take a sip and savour the sweet and sour notes of strawberry, simple syrup, and rum.

Ramon and I got married in 2006, two years after Wallace passed away. Shortly after that, we found out I was pregnant, at thirty-nine years old. I thought I was done having babies, but after marrying Ramon, I wanted nothing more than to give him a child. He had never married or had any children, and I was beyond thrilled to add one more addition to our beautiful family.

We had a baby girl, named Ava. She is the spitting image of Ramon, and she's an absolute ray of sunshine.

A few months after Wallace's death, I put Alaina, Lance, and Maya into therapy to help them through their grief and trauma. They responded well, and ten years later, they continue to thrive. I'm so proud of how well they are doing and everything they've accomplished. However, my mind is occupied now that I have three teenagers and a seven-year-old. The house is full, but I wouldn't have it any other way.

My beautiful and smart Alaina started dating her first boyfriend a little over a year ago. She reminds me a lot of myself. She has that same glow in her dark eyes that I had when I started dating her father. I continue to pray every day that she makes better decisions than I did. So far, it's going well. It's so nice to see her come out of her shell and to watch her confidence grow.

Lance shares many of Wallace's characteristics and mannerisms. He's kind, clever, and talkative. The older he gets, the more he reminds me of the charismatic man his father was. I know he's going to be breaking hearts soon.

Then there's Maya, my mini-me. Not only does she share my features, she also has my strong-willed, slightly stubborn personality. She's ambitious and caring, and I know I'll always be able to count on her.

My children are my entire life, but Ramon keeps my heart full as well. I thought I could never open my heart to love again, but he had already broken down the walls. He gave me the effortless, passionate, beautiful love story I've always dreamed of, and I will never take that for granted.

"Are we heading to Robin's for dinner tonight?" Ramon asks me.

"Yes. She asked us to bring a salad," I reply.

My father passed away in 2008, which is the latest heartbreak I've experienced. I took his death hard. My family grew close after the trauma they experienced with me, and losing him felt like losing the last piece left of the puzzle. We've felt incomplete without him, just like we felt when we lost Mom. However, knowing that he's now reunited with my mother brings us peace.

After Dad passed, Daniel, Robin, and I have made an effort to visit one another regularly. We started weekly dinners with the entire family, each of us taking turns hosting.

Dan and Linda are now grandparents, which makes me feel old. But they are living a wonderfully fulfilled life, and I'm happy for them. Robin and Norman's girls go to school with Lance and Maya, and they have continued to stay close. It feels like everything is exactly where it needs to be.

"When we go to the store for some salad dressing later today, I also need to grab some supplies for the field trip with my students next week," I remind Ramon.

"Oh, yes. Of course, hon." He kisses my forehead, and I smile up at him.

I'm back at the school where Mike and Vic teach. Before returning from my leave after Wallace died, the school board told me that my old school was "not the right fit" after I stood up for myself against the principal. I'm glad I got the chance to leave because I despised that school, anyway.

Victoria found out she was pregnant when I was in the hospital, but she kept the news from me until a few weeks after Wallace's funeral. I was thrilled for them. They were content with their two beautiful, adopted children, but I know they were overjoyed when they found out. They welcomed a beautiful baby boy named Kalem later that year. They continue to make my job feel like a hobby because we have so much fun teaching together. Vic and I teach the same grade now, so it's been great. Vic and Mike have also grown to like Ramon over the years, so we still manage to go on date nights a few times per month.

Life's had a strange serendipity over the last ten years, but I'm not going to complain.

"Mom!" I hear a voice in the distance, distracting me from my thoughts.

I see Alaina rushing toward us.

"Careful by the pool, babe! I don't want you to slip." I say, laughing.

My smile fades when I see the look of worry on her face. "What's wrong?" I ask.

"It's Lance. Something's wrong with him," she says, out of breath from running across the yard.

"Oh no, is he sick?" Ramon asks.

I'm praying for that possibility, but judging from Alaina's expression, she means something entirely different.

"He's been begging me not to tell you, but I can't keep it from you anymore! I thought he was just going through a slump, but he hasn't acted like himself in weeks," she says, exasperated. Tears form in her eyes.

Oh no.

I can't bring myself to speak.

"He refuses to get out of bed. I don't know what to do, Mom."

My breath quickens, and my palms begin to sweat. I feel my heart pounding out of my chest. This can't be, but I'm afraid there can be no other explanation.

The darkness has found its way back.

Acknowledgments

I always knew I had extraordinary people in my life, but I never realized the extent of it until I wrote this book. There are many people I want to recognize and thank for their outstanding support and love during this incredible journey of writing a story that I hold so dearly to my heart. I may not be able to mention everyone, but you all know who you are. Thank you for believing in me. I love and appreciate every single one of you.

Dad, thank you for encouraging and supporting me, and for blessing me with creative genes. I wouldn't have been able to write a story like this without you. Thank you for allowing me to be inspired by some of the vulnerable moments you've experienced. Together, I hope we'll spread awareness about the importance of mental health and help those with similar struggles feel seen.

Anyssa and Liam, my siblings, I can't put into words how your reactions after reading my story for the first time made me feel. I could tell this book was healing for both of you, and being able to provide that is a gift.

Anyssa, thank you for listening to me for hours on end and sharing my excitement for this book. Thank you for believing in me and supporting me through it all. You have no idea how much it means to me. You're my best friend.

Liam, thank you for telling everyone you know about this book the second I gave you the approval. Thank you for being my number one marketing guy. However, it's not just the promotion of my book that I appreciate but also the genuine excitement and pride you've shown. It warms my heart, and I'm so grateful for you.

My niece Maya, you are a ray of sunshine. You may be too young to read this kind of book, but you have been so excited for me. You are remarkably loving. I hope I am making you proud. Je t'aime, mon beau bébé.

My niece Ava, my little sweetheart. You are too young to know that I wrote a book, but I know I will have your full support once you are old enough to understand. You add so much joy to my life. Je t'aime, ma belle Aves.

Matante Rachelle, I know I must've gotten my love of reading from you. You've always embraced my creative side. I knew that the moment you heard about my book, I would have your full support. Thank you for being an important part of this story.

Ashley, the second I gave you the first rough draft of my manuscript, you put your life aside to read it. You've shown me and this story so much love. That kind of support is invaluable. Thank you for your kindness and for supporting me through and through. I will always feel close to you.

Shirley, my fifth cousin and dear friend, you were among the first people with whom I shared my story. Thank you for being my number one fan. Your reaction after reading my book was one of my biggest motivations throughout this process. You made me believe my story was worth sharing. Thank you.

Maddy, you are one of my closest friends. Your excitement and support have been a real gift. I value our friendship so much. Thank you for being there for me since the moment we met.

Lara, thank you for taking the time to read my story. Although our friendship is fairly new, I feel close to you from how much we've shared with one another. You are such a kind and sweet person. I'm looking forward to seeing our friendship continue to grow.

To the rest of my wonderful family and friends who have known about this book and supported me through this process, thank you. You've all had such a positive impact on me, and you've all played a role in helping me accomplish this dream. I appreciate and love every one of you.

Finally, Mom, you are my biggest inspiration and the reason I wrote this book in the first place. I wanted to write a story that would be impactful for you and help you to heal. It was interesting to write a fictional story inspired by your life experiences. Thanks to your storytelling throughout the years, I was capable of crafting this powerful story. I'm beyond grateful for all of the sacrifices you've made for us and the unconditional love you continue to pour out every single day. I hope you can see the significance of your presence in my life. Your perseverance, your empathy, and your power never go unnoticed. It's because of you that I can reach for the stars. I'll spend the rest of my life thanking you for shaping me into the person I am today. I love you so much, Mom.